THE Boy PROJECT

(Notes and Observations of Kara McAllister)

KAMI KINARD

Scholastic Press
New York

250 INDEX CARDS

*For PSM, JPM,
and CLM*

Gr 5+

ISBN 978-0-545-34515-6

12 11 10 9 8 7 6 5 4 3 2 1   12 13 14 15 16/0

Printed in the U.S.A.   23
First printing, January 2012
Book design by Whitney Lyle and Kristina Iulo
Illustration page 5 © Kami Kinard
Illustration of Kara, page 152 © Erin Maguire
Illustration of cars, page 152 © iStockphoto
Illustrations page 202 © iStockphoto

```
THE SCIENTIFIC METHOD:

an organized way of finding
answers to our questions
(according to Ms. Sabatino)

Step 1: Ask a Question

Question: How can I find a boyfriend?
```

Monday, January 1
Bedtime

I am starting this experiment because I have no choice. Well, I have no choice unless you consider being a lifelong boyfriendless social outcast destined to die alone a choice. Which it isn't.

To be honest with you, I probably would have acted sooner if I'd known how truly desperate my situation was. Which I didn't.

I was really in the dark about it. As dark as the closet I went into with Chip Tyler last night after he spun the bottle and it pointed to me.

Chip Tyler is a total dweeb. I've known him since kindergarten. I've grown up a lot since then. Chip hasn't. So I wasn't exactly hoping that I would end up in the closet with Chip on New Year's Eve, but I guess I was a little excited that I might *finally* find out what it feels like to be kissed. But no. As soon as he shut the door behind us, he took my hand in his. Then he shook it. That's all.

I'm not exactly glamorous, but it seems like Chip Tyler would jump at the chance to kiss anything with lips. I'm kind of outraged, to tell the truth, that he thought he was too good to kiss *me*. (Sometimes you have to be outraged to keep from getting hurt.) I mean, what girl walks away from a game of spin the bottle with a handshake? A handshake!

Even Tabbi, my slightly plump, slightly spacey BFF finally got to experience lip-to-lip contact when she went into the closet with James Powalski, whose parents have apparently lost their senses of smell. If they hadn't, they'd have invested a few bucks in sticks of deodorant waaaaay back in sixth grade. Seriously.

But Tabs, who was completely thrilled by the experience, said his BO didn't bother her because you don't breathe all that much when kissing anyway. Right. Now she's an expert.

Being jealous of Tabbi and her one-minute kiss with someone who smells worse than my dad's genuine lamb's wool slippers (which at this point have both the appearance and aroma of roadkill) is a new low for me.

When I came home after that disaster of a party, it hit me like a broom handle whacking a piñata: I've never had a boyfriend—not even the holding-hands variety—and *practically everyone else* has. And it probably wasn't the healthiest thing to do for my self-esteem, but I made a list. Then created a chart. I didn't like the way they turned out at all.

The Boyfriend Status of Girls in My Class

If they've had at least one BF (any grade, even first, like Tabbi), it counts.

Girls in my class	YES	NO
1. Anna	x	
2. Gina	x	
3. Colleen	x	
4. Tiffany	x	
5. Tabbi	x	
6. Dianna	x	
7. Rosemarie	x	
8. Sara	x	
9. Athena	x	
10. Mona	x	
11. La Tisha	x	
12. Gabrielle	x	
13. Jodi	x	
14. Kara (me)		x

Here's what that looks like on a pie chart.

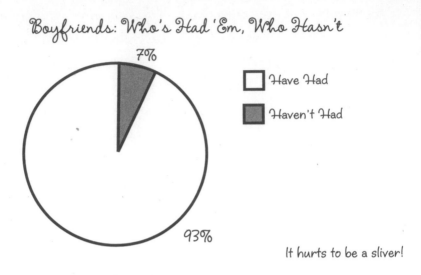

Boyfriends: Who's Had 'Em, Who Hasn't

7%

☐ Have Had

■ Haven't Had

93%

It hurts to be a sliver!

I know that making lists and charts is kinda geeky, but I faced the fact that I *am* kinda geeky a long time ago. How could I avoid coming to that conclusion when every adult in my life keeps telling me I'm smart, nice, and artistic? Smart, nice, artistic girls recognize these compliments as things adults can say when they *can't* say you're pretty, graceful, or cute — and they're too polite to say the opposite. Unfortunately, when you're twelve, being smart is small consolation for being the ONLY girl in your class who's never had a boyfriend.

To make matters worse, I'm also the only person in my ENTIRE family who has never been kissed.

The McAllister Family

Homemade necklace

Perpetual ponytail

Single-handedly trying to resurrect the bow tie. →

Art supplies

↑ Bargain shoes. These are bright green suede.

↑ Practical Danskos. Artsy but comfy.

↑ Expensive track shoes

↑ Flip-flops

BORN 2 RUN

I drew this picture of us in the stick-figure-rear-window-decal style, thinking I'd convince Dad to let us put one on the car like everyone else in America. My plan didn't work. "No good can come out of the general public knowing that two young ladies ride around in this particular vehicle," Dad said.

I think he's wrong about that. I think *a lot* of good can come out of it, especially if some of the single males in the general public notice it and decide to follow our car! What's wrong with a little advertising? It's not like I want to put a BABES ON BOARD sign in the back window!

Anyway, I was just pointing out that EVERYONE else in my family has been kissed. And, okay, it's a given that all parents have kissed and more. (Not that I want to think about that!) But do I have to have a cute older sister who's left a trail of boyfriends in her dust ever since second grade?

It's not fair! Particularly because Julie and I actually kinda look alike. We really do! People are always saying stuff like "You two have *got* to be sisters." It's kind of funny, but they act like they've just solved a big old mystery worthy of Sherlock Holmes when really they just glanced at us and noticed some similarities. Neither of us has straight hair, for example, but Julie's hair is usually described as wavy. Actually, since she keeps it in a perpetual ponytail, it's more like one big curving swoop. My hair, on the other hand, is often described as frizzy. Like clown hair. Or a witch's broom.

And lucky Julie got Dad's green eyes. Mom tries to fool me into thinking *I'm* the lucky one because my eyes are "the best of both worlds," meaning I got some of Dad's green and some of Mom's brown. Most people describe this color as *hazel*, which is a word for green with brown dots flecked in it. Like mud.

So while I admit that I'm not exactly as cute as Julie, at least I'm similarly cute. Plus, sisters have something like 99.9 percent of the exact same DNA! And Julie is obviously attractive to the opposite sex, so I must be at least 99.9 percent as attractive. Since she's had tons of boyfriends, it only stands to reason that I'd have had at least one.

Unfortunately, it looks like reason has very little to do with having boyfriends.

There has to be a *scientific explanation* for this!

See, I know all about scientific explanations. After all, Ms. Sabatino started blabbing about the "scientific method" back in December so we could "use the whole winter break to work on our science fair projects." Come on. They aren't due until February. Even geek girls don't use vacation time to study stuff like velocity. (Unless the experiment involves measuring how fast a desperate girl can run toward a cute boy.)

Still, I was trying to pay really close attention in science before the break, because Mom and Dad said if I could pull off all A's this semester, they'd get me unlimited texting! Apparently they "can't comprehend" how I can have A's in my other classes, and a C in science.

"You love reading," my dad said. "Science is just reading and memorizing."

The man has a point. But he doesn't get that I read because I want to *escape to* all kinds of cool places. Science is one of those places I'd like to *escape from*.

I try to concentrate, I really do. I sit there dutifully taking notes with my brain train chugging along just fine toward some place like Destination Understanding Plant Life. Then Ms. Sabatino will mention some word like *chloroplasts* and it's like she's thrown a switch. All of a sudden my engine is steaming off in another direction, like to Destination How to Make a Bracelet from Plumbing Hardware.

But luckily when Ms. S talked about the science fair this year, she used a word that I always tune in to: *project*. And when she said that word, I suddenly imagined myself winning the entire science fair! Then I realized that if I could bring home that big blue ribbon, it would practically *guarantee* me an A in science, therefore unlimited texting! So I made it my New Year's resolution to WIN the Spring Valley Middle School science fair!

That was two weeks ago.

Now I am officially abandoning this resolution.

My new, more important resolution is this: I, Kara McAllister, will change my image before the end of the school year. By "change my image" I mean "get a boyfriend." And I know exactly how I'm going to do it:

I'll apply both my smart-girl brains and the scientific method to the project. Hey, if the scientific method helped real scientists figure out the structure of an atom, surely it can help me figure out how to find a boyfriend!

Ms. Sabatino made us write down the steps of the scientific method so we'd be able to follow them for our science fair projects. I copied them onto a note card, then taped it in here so I wouldn't lose it.

THE SCIENTIFIC METHOD

Step 1: Ask a Question
Step 2: Do Background Research
Step 3: Form a Hypothesis
Step 4: Test Your Hypothesis
Step 5: Interpret Your Data
Step 6: Draw a Conclusion
Step 7: Publish Results
Step 8: Retest

The small size of index cards makes them perfect for inconspicuously taking notes on my subjects (boys) in their natural setting (school). The scientific term for this is *unobtrusive observation*. To tell the truth, I was glad to learn that this was a real method, because I was pretty much going to use this strategy anyway. What method of research could *possibly* be easier? All you have to do is be a little sly while looking around and make sure not to gawk or anything. Hopefully my observations will help me figure out what I need to do to change my status.

Piece of cake!

I'll be the seventh-grade version of Jane Goodall, except I'll be observing boys instead of chimps. Not that there's a huge difference.

Tuesday, January 2
First period

THE SCIENTIFIC METHOD

Step 2: Do Background Research

(Let the unobtrusive observations begin!)

I arrived at school today armed with index cards, my pen, this journal, and the determination to get a social life. Or at least a boyfriend.

DIY Boyfriend-Finding Kit

So it was pretty hard to concentrate while Mrs. Willis was lecturing about the Civil War. Again. Today the topic was General Lee at Gettysburg. I was looking around at the guys in my class and taking mental notes while she talked.

Now that I'm observing them as a researcher, I'm noticing things that I've never noticed before. Malcolm Maxwell was doodling on his Chucks the *entire* time Mrs. Willis was talking, for example. Does he do that every day? I wouldn't know. I am usually paying *way* too much attention to what the teacher is saying.

I also noticed Chip Tyler putting tiny pieces of paper into the curly hair of Dianna Leroy. See how mature he is? The back of her head was practically white, but she didn't seem to feel a thing. It was weirdly fascinating to watch. A lot of other people seemed to think so, too.

When Mrs. W finished talking, she made us write three paragraphs from the point of view of a soldier following Lee as he retreated back to Virginia. I turned in my paper first.

Normally, I'd pull out whatever book I'm trying to escape into at this point. This week it happens to be *Bras and Broomsticks*, which is a book about a girl whose little sister is a witch. A real one. But the good kind. Anyway, the older sister wants to improve her social life, so she convinces her kid sis to use her magical powers to help. What I wouldn't give for a sister with useful skills like that! But since I'm stuck with Julie, whose only skill seems to be making me look like the second-best sister, I am forced to take matters into my own hands. Which meant it was time to seriously study. Study boys.

I looked around. Who should be my very first subject? Cool Phillip Bernard? Nice Evan Carlson? Handsome Alex Brantley?

"Kara McAllister! Keep your eyes on your own paper!" snapped Mrs. W.

What? She thought I was cheating?! I politely told her I'd already turned in my paper.

"Then get out a book and read. Stop looking around at your friends." Everyone did the stare-at-whoever-is-being-yelled-at thing, so my face started heating up like it does when I eat Mouth of Hades chili at Texas Steakranch. In my head I could hear Lee yelling, "Retreat! Retreat!" But there wasn't anywhere for me to go.

So much for unobtrusive observation.

Thankfully, Dianna stood up just then and a blizzard of paper snow fell from her head. That drew attention away from me in a big way. Poor Dianna.

Third period

I was trying to be objective about which guy to study first, but I think, deep down, I already knew it'd be Evan Carlson.

I've known him since kindergarten and have had a crush on him for months.

What's *really great* about Evan is that, even though he's gotten a lot cuter over the past year, he's just as nice as ever. (Not like *some* people, who, once they start getting a little attention, act like they never used to play tag with you every single day.) Evan still looks right at me with his big gray eyes when we talk, and he has this gorgeous smile, even if he does wear braces.

Since Evan *is* so nice, it makes me wonder: WHY DON'T I HAVE THE GUTS TO GO TALK TO HIM? I am NEVER going to find a boyfriend if I can't even make myself talk to a nice guy I've known for over seven years!

At least I'll have an excuse to study him now. I pulled out a note card and jotted down my observations, and then taped it in here for safekeeping.

Subject #1: EVAN CARLSON
Data Collected on: 1/2   Status: Available
Hair: Sandy blond
Eyes: Gray
Eyebrows: Average
Body Type: OK — has small love handles
Age: 12
Nice-o-meter: ☺☺☺☺☺
Interest Level: ♥♥♥♥♥

Bedtime (According to my parents, not me)

I managed to gather some more data today. This was because we had a sub in third period, which pretty much meant we could do whatever we wanted. Quietly. And I wanted to do some unobtrusive observing.

I slumped down in my chair, pulled the hood of my hoodie over my head, and held my index cards under my desk so I could write without anyone seeing. It worked! No one noticed me at all. I was so successful at going unnoticed that it was kind of depressing. . . .

I figured since I made *my* crush Subject #1, I should make Tabbi's crush Subject #2, even though she is wasting her time longing for the totally unobtainable Alex Brantley. He's the best-looking boy in school. And guys like that never go for girls like Tabbi. I'm not being mean! He wouldn't go for a girl like me, either. It's like he's a different species or something.

Subject #2: ALEX BRANTLEY

Data Collected on: 1/2   Status: TAKEN!

Hair: Black and thick

Eyes: Brown

Eyebrows: Perfect

Body Type: Athletic

Age: 13

Nice-o-meter: ☺☺☺

Interest Level: ♥♥

(True confession: I'd totally be more interested if I thought I had a chance.)

Besides, even if he did show interest in Tabbi, it wouldn't do her any good because Alex's girlfriend, Colleen, will claw the eyes out of anyone who comes between them. She has the nails to do it, too. Trust me. They're long, gorgeous, and manicured. My nails have never looked that good! The only thing I've ever managed to get a good coat of nail polish on was a wooden pencil. I have to admit, it did jazz it up! Especially after I stuck those little rhinestones around the eraser. There's something super-satisfying about transforming an everyday object like a pencil into a fabulous writing tool.

I guess Colleen feels the same way about her nails. You can tell she's proud of them because she's always clicking them together, drawing attention to how glam they are. Tabbi and I make up names for girls like Colleen and when it came to picking her name, I was arguing for "Keyboard." All that nail clicking makes it sound like she's constantly typing.

But Tabbi said "Maybelline" was more appropriate because in addition to wearing perfect polish, Colleen also wears a ton of makeup. Not that she needs it. She's really pretty. She actually needs makeup *less* than the rest of us . . . but she wears *more* of it. Her lips are always rosy. Her eyelids—pale green. Tabbi claimed the name Maybelline covered the nails AND face, but Keyboard only the nails. I guess she's right. It wouldn't matter if she wasn't though. She never backs down.

Speaking of Tabbi, she's calling now. . . .

Bedtime. I admit it.

Just got off the phone, but only because Tabbi's mom came and yanked hers out of her hand. She's waaaay strict about bedtime.

Tabbi and I had the usual conversation. It always goes something like this:

Tabs: Do you think he'll dump her?

Me: No.

Tabs: Ever?

Me: Nope.

Tabs: But he's been with her since fifth grade. Don't you think one day he'll wake up and see how awful she is?

Me: Tabs, guys like that don't try to see more than the surface. Maybelline may be mean, but she's gorgeous.

Tabs: (*Groan*) So is he.

Me: I know.

And I do know. I spent a long time observing Alex out of the corner of my eye today. (It's the only way you *can* look at him because Maybelline is super-jealous and she sits right behind me in most classes since her last name is McCarver.) Alex is stunningly, deliciously gorgeous. If he were a movie star, big-time directors would say stuff like this about him: *I must have Alex Brantley for that role so thousands of girls will pay to see my wonderful movie over and over and over just to look at him. Then my film will be a box-office hit and I'll win an Academy Award!* I can see why Tabbi likes to dream about him. But it's only a dream.

Tabs: *Sigh.* He's such a nice person.

Me: Nice, yes. But have you ever noticed that he doesn't look at girls like us the way he looks at Maybelline?

Tabs: Meaning . . .

Me: I always feel like he's looking at me like I'm something absolutely boring. Like a chair. Or a dictionary.

Tabs: I'm pretty sure he doesn't look at me that way!

Me: Uh-huh.

Tabs: He's perfect.

Me: Not.

Tabs: Name one thing about him that isn't perfect.

Me: Maybelline.

Tabs: Besides her.

Me: He chews gum NONSTOP. I've heard the bottom of his desk has so much gum stuck to it that it'd bounce like a superball if you threw it down on the sidewalk.

(I think I could overlook the gum chewing though, if I had a chance to date someone like him. Not that I ever will.)

Tabs: I wish I was a piece of gum.

Me: Ewwww.

Tabbi wasted a lot more time talking about Alex, as if talking about him would increase her chances with him. Which it won't. I fell into barely listening and interjecting an "uh-huh" or "yep" every now and then. It was hard to concentrate. Probably because the more she talks about *her* crush, the more I think I should confess mine. But every time I get ready to tell her how I feel about Evan, something holds me back. I guess I don't want to jinx it.

Wednesday, January 3
Early. Too early.

It's still mascara black outside. But I can't go back to sleep after that disturbing dream I just had about James Powalski — the boy Tabbi kissed during the spin the bottle.

It was one of those forgot-my-homework type of dreams. I was scrambling through my locker, tossing papers over my shoulder. Then someone handed me the exact paper I was looking for. I turned around and found myself staring into James Powalski's face. (If you could smell things in your dreams, I'd have known it was him *before* I turned around. Thankfully, though, smells don't creep into dreams.)

James's face isn't monster-terrible or anything. Still, it's pretty disturbing to have someone like him show up in your head when that head is resting on a satiny pillow and attached to a body wearing spaghetti-strap pj's. At first I wondered if my dream meant that I was still jealous about Tabbi's kiss with him. But luckily I realized that he probably just popped up because he's the last guy I took notes on yesterday. I'm going to have to be more careful about who I study last. Here is the card I made for him.

Subject #3: JAMES POWALSKI
Data Collected on: 1/2   Status: Available?
Hair: Wavy and black
Eyes: Brown
Eyebrows: Dark and thick and married in the middle
Body type: Tall and scrawny
Age: 13
Nice-o-meter: ☺☺
Interest Level: 0
Observations: James was passing notes with Gina Johns. (Ewwww)
Fast Fact: His armpits still haven't been introduced to deodorant.

Normally I wouldn't even pay attention to someone like James, but I'm forcing myself to be objective because I want reliable results. Plus, some of the things I don't like about James are fixable.

For example, I heard that all of the guys at the *other* middle school have to line up after gym and reach for the stars. Then the coach goes down the line and sprays every pit with Right Guard. Now, if someone *happened* to leave an anonymous note for Coach Little giving *him* that idea, I'm sure he'd jump on it. He never misses a chance to humiliate us, and standing with your pits exposed is not exactly a confidence-building exercise. So if I ever decided I had a crush on James, I might just have to author such a note. (And forever after, shave my armpits on a daily basis in case Coach Little got the bright idea to give the girls the same treatment.)

But there's one thing about James that I will not be able to change and that thing is going to make him off-limits to me forever. The thing is named Gina Johns. Tabbi and I call her "The Vine" because she's always climbing all over the trunk of some guy or another.

While I was observing James yesterday, I couldn't help noticing that it looks like The Vine was trying to put down roots near him.

Hmmm. I might need to start getting ready for school. It's getting lighter—charcoal gray—outside. Besides, I smell bacon.

Bus stop (AKA my front yard)

Great. The bus is about to stop and here comes Julie breezing by on her bike. I hate when she does that! Because you pretty much suffer in comparison when your cute, athletic older sister (who already went jogging at the crack of dawn) blows by you on two wheels while you're standing as still as a lawn ornament, waiting to board the slowest and most embarrassing form of transportation possible. I'd rather ride a camel to school. Seriously.

First period

Dear Mrs. Willis,

Please stop talking. I'm missing a great opportunity to continue my research. See, I have an awesome view of Phillip Bernard's profile right now. I would very much like to make a few notes about He Who Will Soon Be Known As Subject #4. But if I get out my index cards, it'll call attention to the fact that I'm not taking notes on your lecture. Which I am not.

You are too far away, however, to realize that I use this particular notebook as a journal, so you probably think that I'm writing about General Lee's surrender, when instead I'm writing about the most important thing in the world: finding a boyfriend.

You talk a lot about democracy, Mrs. Willis, but if we took a vote, I'm pretty sure everyone would rather learn about relationships than the Civil War. But we won't take a vote, will we? One thing school has taught me is that American democracy pretty much dies at the classroom door.

It's not that I think Phillip Bernard is "the one for me." But you never know. He does have one feature that I'm really into. His eyebrows! I have a good view of the right one from here. It is perfectly arched—almost like an elf's.

Guys say stuff like "I'm a face man" or "I'm a leg man." (Okay, guys don't really talk like that around me, but I've heard them on TV.) Given the face-man/leg-man thing, I guess I have to say that I'm an eyebrow girl. I always notice a guy's eyebrows.

I think the world is full of closet eyebrow women. If not, how do you explain all of those celebrities with great, unusual, or highly arched eyebrows? Robert Pattinson! Orlando Bloom! Zac Efron! And it can't be mere coincidence that lead singers are usually whichever band member has the best eyebrows. Like Joe Jonas! Anyway, Phillip has some very nice eyebrows. Way better than Evan's, by the way.

Oh, Mrs. Willis. You are still talking. Talking about people who are not eligible to participate in my boyfriend study because they are . . . dead. I'll have to take notes on Phillip later. Thanks a lot.

Signed, but never to be delivered by,
Kara McAllister

P.S. Ha! Was able to get these notes during the last five minutes of class! Your filibuster didn't bust me, Mrs. Willis!

Subject #4: PHILLIP BERNARD
Data Collected on: 1/3   Status: Available
Hair: Longish brown
Eyes: Chocolate
Eyebrows: Perfectly arched — elfish
Body Type: Thin but muscular
Age: 12
Nice-o-meter: ☺☺☺☺☺
Interest Level: ♥♥

Lunch

I had just enough time to update my data on Subject #3 before Tabs joined me.

Subject #3: JAMES POWALSKI (Card 2)
Data Collected on: 1/2   Status: TAKEN!
Hair: Wavy and black
Eyes: Brown
Eyebrows: Dark and thick and married in the middle
Body type: Tall and scrawny
Age: 13
Nice-o-meter: ☺☺
Interest Level: 0
Observations: James was passing notes with Gina Johns. (Ewwww)
Fast Fact: His armpits still haven't been introduced to deodorant.

Yep. James and The Vine are definitely an item! She's giving him a hug right now. He seems to be enjoying it, too. Probably because he's never had a girlfriend before. Not one that I know about, anyway. (Thanks to Tabbi, however, he's an experienced kisser. Apparently.)

Gina, on the other hand, has had so many boyfriends that it absolutely proves one thing: Life isn't fair!

How Life Isn't Fair: Two Charts
by Kara McAllister

These charts show exactly how life isn't fair. Because The Vine keeps having more and more relationships, her growth chart shows a steady increase. But mine is always the same. Stagnant. Dormant. Dead. Can you even call it a chart if nothing changes?

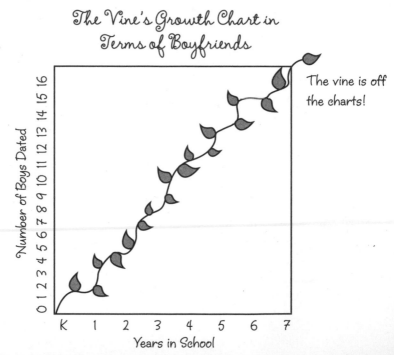

The Vine's Growth Chart in Terms of Boyfriends

The vine is off the charts!

Number of Boys Dated

0 1 2 3 4 5 6 7 8 9 10 11 12 13 14 15 16

K   1   2   3   4   5   6   7

Years in School

My Growth Chart in
Terms of Boyfriends

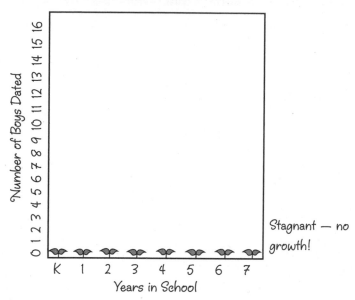

Number of Boys Dated

0 1 2 3 4 5 6 7 8 9 10 11 12 13 14 15 16

Stagnant — no growth!

K 1 2 3 4 5 6 7

Years in School

HOW can The Vine have had so many boyfriends when I haven't had a single one? It's as if bad luck is following me around like that cat in *Bad Kitty*, which is a book about a girl whose life gets pretty crazy after a cat crosses her path.

I mean Gina Johns isn't even that cute. She does what my mom calls "overcompensating." Too much flirting. Too much makeup. Too much giggling. Too much jewelry. She has very black hair. (It was brown last year.) She uses very black eyeliner. And she wears very black boots all the time. Even in summer.

I just don't understand what the attraction is. Well, maybe I do. But I can't be like that. If James likes the kind of girl Gina is, he's definitely off of my list of possibilities!

Homework time (According to my parents)

I didn't have a chance to take notes on anyone else during school. But I was determined NOT to let James Powalski be the last guy I studied. Let's just say I'm hoping for sweet dreams tonight.

So when I heard Chip Tyler laughing in the back of the bus, I decided to focus my powers of unobtrusive observation on him, even though he:

1. is not a huge improvement over James.
2. got on my very last nerve today.
3. cannot possibly be right for me, according to my mimi.

I know Chip isn't right for me because one time I asked my mimi how she knew to pick my grandpa, and she said: *You don't pick who you love the most. You pick who annoys you the least.* Well, if that's the gold standard, I can absolutely strike Chip Tyler off of my list! That boy is *so annoying*. He's the type that taps your left shoulder if he is standing on your right. Then he snickers about it when you turn your head and look into the eyes of . . . no one. Plus, I still can't forgive him for shaking my hand in that closet.

If that isn't enough evidence, what he did during Mrs. Hill's class third period proves that he's the most annoying guy on the planet. Or at least in the seventh grade. Today the sub passed around a sheet for us to sign to prove to Mrs. Hill that we were in class. Lucky for me, Tabbi was the last one to sign it—because she noticed my name wasn't on it. When she passed the paper back to me, I saw that my name had been erased and *Anita Bath* was written in place of it.

Chip was bent over, acting like he was tying his shoe, but I could see his shoulders shaking so I know he's the one who wrote it. Typical. With his head down, I had the perfect chance to erase his name and write *Stu Pitt* instead. I did this quickly, before I could talk myself out of it, then ran the sheet up to the sub.

I really don't think Mrs. Hill will suspect that I wrote the phony name, because I never do anything wrong. Honestly. I'm *that* boring. I hope boring people can find love, too. Never mind. I know they can. Look at my parents.

Subject #5: CHIP TYLER
Data Collected on: 1/3   Status: Single (I'm betting forever.)
Hair: Plain brown
Eyes: Plain brown
Eyebrows: Never noticed
Body Type: Goofy
Age: 12
Nice-o-meter: ☺
Interest Level: 0
Fast Fact: Subject is extremely annoying!

Taking notes on Chip is probably a big waste of time. But it will be worth it if I don't see James in dreamland tonight.

Thursday, January 4
Waiting for first bell to ring

Evan and I were walking into the building at the same time today and he said, "Hi," and I said, "Hi." No big deal, right? Wrong! I'm trying to get up the nerve to talk to him at lunch.

First period. After the test.

I just turned in my test on the Battle of Gettysburg and I figure as long as I look down, Mrs. Willis won't claim I'm not keeping my eyes on my own paper. If she *does* call me out, it'll be totally hypocritical because Tiffany Davidson *never* has her eyes on her own paper. She always has them glued to Alex. Not Alex Brantley. Alex Langford. I took a good long look at him, too, while I was walking back to my seat.

Subject #6: ALEX LANGFORD	
Data Collected on: 1/4	Status: Taken!
Hair: Dark brown	
Eyes: Dark brown	
Eyebrows: Ho-Hum	
Body Type: Ho-Hum	
Age: 12	
Nice-o-meter: ☺☺☺	
Interest Level: 0	
Fatal Flaw: B-O-R-I-N-G	

Alex Langford is like a watered-down version of Alex Brantley—just like his girlfriend, Tiffany, is a watered-down version of Maybelline. Tabbi and I call Tiffany "The

Sponge" because if Colleen is the makeup, then Tiffany is definitely the applicator sponge! She soaks up everything that is Maybelline.

I don't like Maybelline at all, but I have to admit that she has a personality. It's a mean, nasty, vain personality—but no one can deny that she has one.

The Sponge's only personality trait, on the other hand, is that she wants to be just like Maybelline. I mean, if there were a body-size Maybelline tattoo, Tiffany would be tattooed from head to toe. In fact, I think the only reason Tiffany likes Alex Langford is that he has the same first name as Maybelline's boyfriend. She's always talking to Maybelline about "*my* Alex and *your* Alex."

Anyway, Alex Langford doesn't have much of a personality either. All he does is stand around next to Alex Brantley with his arm around The Sponge, smiling at what *other* people say. So it's fine with me if he's The Sponge's boyfriend. I just don't want someone like that for mine.

Homework time (According to my parents) Daydream time (According to me)

I love my room. Last summer, Mom said I could "celebrate my creativity" by decorating it any way I wanted (within reason). And despite the fact that I think it is perfectly reasonable to paint a ceiling black before covering it with glow-in-the-dark stars and Mom does not, I like how my room turned out. We bought this thick, shaggy cream rug, and Mom helped me make cool roll-down shades out of old jeans. (The really great thing about those is that I can store small things that I don't want Mom to see in the pockets. Like notes. And no, they don't fall out.)

Dad helped, too, by covering the old pink walls with indigo paint. We strung little Christmas lights around the crown molding for the finishing touch. So even though I was vetoed on the black-ceiling thing, I still have the feeling of being wrapped in a night sky when I roll down the shades, turn off the overhead lights, and relax on my cloudlike, fluffy shag rug, looking up at the twinkling Christmas-light stars.

Because my room *is* so cool, I never really mind going there to study. Or to do things that are more important than studying. Like trying to figure out how to get a boyfriend.

What I mostly want to figure out right now is how I can get Evan Carlson to ask me out. I think I'm getting a little closer to that goal! Today at lunch I casually suggested to Tabbi that instead of sitting at our usual table with Anna Johnstone and Dianna Leroy, we sit at Evan's table. It's right next to the "popular" table, where Alex Brantley and Maybelline sit, along with their ever-present groupies, Alex Langford and The Sponge. Tabbi thought it was a great idea!

I felt a little guilty using Tabbi's obsession with the unobtainable to obtain my obsession. But we ended up having a great conversation with Evan! Tabbi even stopped drooling over Alex B long enough to join in the discussion, thank goodness, because I was having a hard time thinking of stuff to say. I let Tabs do most of the talking until the conversation turned to track.

Evan wants to join the team this spring. He's even going to weight training after school. Luckily, this is a subject I know something about, being the sister of a track star and all. Who knew those hundreds of butt-numbing hours on metal bleachers would come in handy?

So. I may not have found a boyfriend, but at least I've found the courage to approach my crush!

Friday, January 5
Lunch

There is no one—NO ONE—left in the cafeteria. And I wouldn't be here either except that if a teacher keeps you in for lunch detention, they're obligated to let you out for at least the last ten minutes so you have a chance to eat. You read that right. Detention.

This was my first experience with detention ever, and it was totally mortifying. It turns out that Mrs. Hill *is* capable of suspecting a completely boring student who *never* gets in trouble of creatively altering an attendance sheet. Actually, the detention itself wasn't so mortifying. But what Mrs. Hill said in front of the whole entire class was. I'll never forget those words.

"Kara and Chip need to stay seated when the bell rings. The two of you have lunch detention for that little stunt you pulled yesterday."

Thankfully, the *brrrriiiiiiiiiiing* cut her off.

Did you know that out of a class of twenty-three students, eighteen look back over their shoulders when they leave a room? At least they do when two of their classmates are in trouble. Tabbi gave me a sympathetic backward glance. She was the only one who knew that we were guilty of what Mrs. Hill later called "tampering with the substitute's role." Everyone else just seemed curious. Even Evan. ☹

Who Is Capable of Minding Their Own Business?

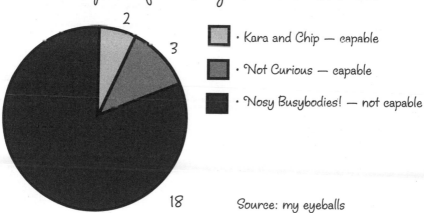

2

3

- Kara and Chip — capable
- Not Curious — capable
- Nosy Busybodies! — not capable

18

Source: my eyeballs

See how many nosy people there are in my class? See?

Will this ruin my chances with Evan? *Stunt* could mean anything. What if he thinks Chip and I were kissing or something? What if he's incapable of loving someone who's served detention? I felt sick.

I felt even sicker when Mrs. Hill told us our punishment was to "talk and discover something to like about each other." Then she left the room!

As soon as she was gone, Chip said, "What'd you replace my name with—*Justin Credible*?"

"No," I said. "I went with *Stu Pitt*. But I should have used *Yul B. Sari*."

"Actually, *Jed I. Knight* would have been perfect." (Apparently he's a huge Star Wars fan. Figures.)

"Nah," I said. "But *Ima Moron* suits."

Chip suggested a few more names. So did I. The more crazy names we came up with, the funnier it got.

We eventually made a list of twenty-three names. One for each of the students in our class. Next time we have a sub, we're going to replace the entire class list with our bogus list.

By the time Mrs. Hill came back, we were cracking ourselves up. She gave us what mystery writers call a "knowing smile" and said, "It's just as I suspected. You two have solved your differences!"

I don't know about solving our differences. I guess I

think Chip Tyler is pretty funny now. I mean, I still think he makes a lot of stupid jokes, but he makes some funny ones, too.

The bell is ringing and I haven't eaten a bite!

After school

Tabbi called me as soon as the bus pulled up in front of my house. That girl has perfect timing. She knows I can't really talk about anything good when I'm trapped in the guts of the big yellow land whale. We didn't have the usual conversation. Unfortunately.

Tabs: So? Detention was about the fake names you guys put on the sub list, right?

Me: Yep. Thanks for passing the list back to me, BTW. You could've just turned it in. Then only Chip would've gotten in trouble.

Tabs: (*Giggles*) Sorry! I thought you'd want to know.

Me: (*Sigh*) I did.

Tabs: So what'd you have to do?

Me: Nothing.

Tabs: You're kidding. You didn't clean desks, write paragraphs, or anything?

Me: Nope.

Tabs: What'd Mrs. H say to you?

Me: Well, she said we needed to talk and work out our differences. Then she left the room.

Tabs: No! She left you alone with Chip Tyler? That *is* a punishment!

Me: He wasn't so bad, actually.

Tabs: Not so bad?! How can you say that about that knucklehead? Wait a minute. Please tell me he didn't try to make up for that spin the bottle goof-up. Did you guys kiss?

Me: TAB-I-THA!

Tabs: KA-RA!

Me: I wouldn't kiss Chip Tyler.

Tabs: You went into that closet with him. . . .

Me: That was different and you know it. It was dark, and we were at a party. And it was a game. I had to go into the closet with him when the bottle pointed to me or else look like a dork.

Tabs: So why'd you say he wasn't bad?

Me: He's just funny. That's all.

Tabs: Oh.

Me: (*Trying to change the subject*) Sorry I abandoned you at lunch. Who'd you end up sitting with?

Tabs: Evan.

Me:

Me:

Me:

Tabs: Kara? Hello?

Me: I thought you liked Alex!

(I kind of shrieked that last sentence. Hope Tabs didn't notice.)

Tabs: I do. But I can't exactly sit with him while Maybelline is all over him. And Evan was so nice yesterday, I thought I'd just sit there again.

Me: (*Trying to sound casual*) Was he nice again today?

Tabs: Sure. And I had a great view of Alex the whole time.

Me: (*Huge sigh of relief that I hope Tabs didn't hear*) Do you think Alex noticed you?

Tabs: Yeah, but he couldn't really talk to me. You know. He has to pretend to like Maybelline.

Me: Tabs. He does like Maybelline.

Tabs: How could he? She's so mean. Do you think he'll dump her?

Me: No.

Tabs: Ever?

Me: Nope.

And we talked about Tabs's obsession until Mom called me for dinner. Whew!

Bedtime (According to my parents, even though tomorrow is SATURDAY!)

Ugh! It's the weekend, and weekends = doom. I know, because I did the equation.

2 whole days without seeing Evan
+ 0 chance to see other guys unless they're visiting Julie
1 very long weekend

Sunday, January 7
Late afternoon. Or evening. I'm not sure which.

With no one to unobtrusively observe, I couldn't exactly move forward with my research. So I headed to the "family computer located in a high-traffic area" and Googled *boyfriend*, just to see if there was any data online about the topic. Apparently there is. Unfortunately, a lot of it's blocked by research-inhibiting-net-nanny software. Thanks, Dad.

But I did find one site that was really interesting. It's called *Bebe Truelove's 10-Week Guide to Finding a Soul Mate*. There's a photo of Bebe on the home page. She has flowing red hair, plump shiny lips, and a great figure. According to her, a soul mate is the one person in the world who understands you completely and shares your hopes and dreams.

Reading this, I realized I've been selling myself short! I've spent the past week trying to figure out how to get a boyfriend when what I really need to be looking for is that one person who completes me! I think I need to modify my research. I took out my journal and added the word *SOUL* above the word *Observations*.

```
THE SCIENTIFIC METHOD

Step 1: Ask a Question

Question: How can I find my one and only
              soul mate?
```

Maybe it won't be too hard for me to find my soul mate now that I've discovered Bebe Truelove. She has an uncanny knack for helping soul mates unite! There was even a heart in the right-hand corner of the screen with the number 487 in it, which is the current number of people who've found their one and only soul mate, using Bebe's advice.

The rest of the screen was filled with testimonials from her former clients, and instructions for how to get her advice.

"I followed Bebe's advice and met Martin in only 2 weeks!" —*R. Purcell*
"Bebe's tips make finding love easy." —*Alexis Alexander*
"Signing up for Bebe's e-mails is the best thing I've ever done." —*Sonya Smith*

I signed up. Hey, it couldn't hurt! Getting tips from experts might be just the background research I need for this experiment. I think Ms. Sabatino would even call Bebe a "primary source," since Bebe knows so much about the topic of love.

There was a *ping* almost immediately and a red flag started waving from the mailbox at the bottom of my screen. Bebe had already sent me the first tip! (And an ad for Love-Mist body spray, whatever that is.)

To: Kara M <Craftychick@mailquickly.com>
From: BebeTruelove <bebe@bebetruelove.com>
Subject: Tip #1

Dear Soul Mate Seeker,

A guy likes a girl who is true to herself. If you like yourself, he'll like you back!

40

Tip #1: Be yourself.

Good Luck in Love,

Bebe

Come on, Bebe! That's the lamest advice I've ever received. I've been being myself for the past twelve years, and look where it's gotten me. Nowhere!!!! I felt like clicking on UNSUBSCRIBE right then and there. But something held me back. Something called curiosity. Or desperation. I'm not sure which.

WEEK 1: RESEARCH REVIEW
# of subjects unobtrusively observed: 6

Findings: Some guys like popular girls.
Some guys like clingy girls. No guys like me.

Most significant finding: My courage.
I actually sat with Evan!

Bebe Truelove's Tip #1: Be yourself.
(Already proven NOT to work!)

Data Collection Methods: observation, Internet

Monday, January 8
Fourth period

Finally, I had few a minutes of free time during fourth period to take notes on the most obviously perfect guy in that class. The teacher himself! Mr. Steven DeLacey.

We don't usually get free time in Mr. DeLacey's class because he works us like dogs. (Question: When people say "worked us like dogs," do they mean sled dogs? Those are the only kind of working dogs I can think of. And really, it's not like he makes us run through miles of snow or anything. Not that I wouldn't run through miles of snow for Mr. DeLacey. I totally would. Even if I don't have a thick coat of hair, padded paws, and wolves for ancestors.)

Anyway, the point is that no one minds working hard for Mr. DeLacey because he's cute. And I'm not the only girl who's noticed.

Mr. DeLacey has about half of the class wishing they were a decade older. The other half is male. And he has all of us wanting to understand algebra well enough to impress him. His eyes are really big and nice. When he's explaining something, he looks right at you with those huge blue eyes and says, "Do you get it now?" In those particular moments, I'm never thinking about algebra. I just nod my head and know that my mom is going to have to do a lot of explaining to me when I get home.

Subject #7: MR. DELACEY
Data Collected on: 1/8   Status: Available
Hair: Brown
Eyes: Pale blue
Eyebrows: Thin
Body Type: Mannish (But without a gut like Dad's)
Age: 23
Nice-o-meter: ☺☺☺☺☺
Interest Level: ♥♥♥♥♥ (Interest level has been accelerated by 10 years.)

It might seem crazy to write about someone who's eleven years older than me. But I like to look at it this way: My grandpa is ten years older than my mimi. So even though right now I'm sure Mr. DeLacey wouldn't consider dating a seventh grader, someday I'll be twenty-one and he'll be thirty-three. That isn't so bad, is it? The point is, again, you never know.

Obviously Mr. DeLaccy is too old to be my boyfriend. But what if we were meant to be together, you know, eternally? Now that I've visited Bebe Truelove's site, I can't help thinking that Mr. DeLacey would make a great soul mate. One thing he has going for him is that he already knows how to solve for *x*. *X* being an unknown answer. You just have to know how to use the information right in front of you to find it. Kind of like finding a soul mate.

Fifth period

We're supposed to be writing notes about our science fair projects. Luckily (for my science grade, but not for my social life) I had all weekend free with nothing better to do than try to complete that pesky assignment. The problem was that every time I tried to think of a good topic, I ended up daydreaming about Evan.

Then a sweet idea hit me like a ton of candy corn: I could use my *real* science fair project as an excuse to gather information for my secret, and more important, *soul mate* research project. I mean, I could even conduct a survey or something that gives me super–relationship insight! That would be awesome.

So I spent the next few hours consulting the most authoritative sources on boyfriends out there: teen magazines! I dug around under Julie's bed until I uncovered a stack of old mags like *G-16*, *Astroteen*, and *Drama Tween*. (Julie hides all the things she thinks make her look immature under her bed. I found fifteen Webkinz and three empty Big League Chew bags there, too.)

Anyway, once I discovered the magazines, I began some serious research. Like marking all of the pages that had surveys and quizzes on them. I stuck blue sticky notes on personality-type quizzes like "What Color Are You?" and "What Does Your Room Say About You?" and "Which Character from

_____ *(fill in the blank with title of block-buster movie)* Are You?" I didn't know you could tell so much about a person by looking at what kind of junk they have on their desk, what kind of doodles they draw, or what type of eye makeup they wear!

I stuck pink notes to the pages that had quizzes about crushes, like "Should You Act Flirty or Not?" and "Can You Decode Guy Talk?" and "Are You a Butterfly (Social) or Flower (Wall)?" I even found a quiz called "Does Your Crush Like You Back?" I couldn't resist filling it out. I kinda wish I hadn't, though. The quiz was set up like a flow chart. It started with a question in a box. A *yes* arrow led one direction and a *no* arrow another. Depending on which arrows you picked as you answered the questions, you eventually ended up in one of three boxes at the bottom of the page:

- Yes! You Go, Girl!
- He's Noticed You, Keep Trying
- No! Time to Move On

Well, guess which box I ended up in.

But even though the quiz didn't work out the way I wanted, it did give me an idea for a great science fair project that will also help me with my boy research.

First I created a personality survey for the girls by mixing my own burning questions with questions I pulled from different personality quizzes. Based on how they answer the questions, my female classmates will be divided into three separate types:

Type A: Insecure/Clingy
Type B: Artistic/Independent
Type C: Popular/Snobby

Then I created a box-and-arrow flow-chart quiz to lead guys through a path of questions that will reveal which one of the three types of girls they like! Since I'll be one of the types of girls the boys can pick, I'll be able to see which boys in my class answer the questions that lead to *my* letter. This is what my dad would call a hidden agenda, which is a plan that is kept secret. A stealth plan. The kind a spy would make.

Needless to say, it is the hidden agenda part of the experiment that I'm most excited about. And it rocks that I found one experiment that will support two different hypotheses, which are unproven theories, according to Ms. S.

#1: Official Science Fair Hypothesis

Based on interest surveys, I think boys will prefer one type of girl over other types.

AND

#2: Hidden Agenda Hypothesis

Finding out which boys are attracted to my type of girl will help me see which ones are most likely to have boyfriend potential or, better yet, soul-mate potential!

Here's the most fabulous thing about the whole project: When I asked Mr. DeLacey if I could distribute the surveys during algebra, he said, "Sure." Then he offered to give them to the rest of his math sections because he said research is always more accurate when you have a "larger sample"! He even said he'd take one *himself*! How lucky is that? So now I'll have data on 115 people, about half of them guys. This is awesome! Now I just need to go fill out one of Ms. Sabatino's science fair applications, staple copies of the quizzes to it, and I'm home free!!!!

Student Name: _Kara McAllister_ **Teacher Name:** _Ms. Sabatino_

Grade Level: _8_ **Class Period:** _5th_

Level (select one)

☒ individual ☐ small group ☐ class project

Scientific Category

☐ life science ☐ physical science ☐ engineering

☒ behavioral science ☐ earth and space science

Project Title: _Matching Attractions_

What is the question that your project will answer?

Do 8th-grade boys prefer a certain type of girl?

State your hypothesis:

Based on interest surveys, I think boys will prefer one type of girl over other types.

Materials Used:

paper, pencils, computer (for typing)

Survey for Girls

Directions: Please circle the letter that best completes the scientific research statement.

1. If I have an hour of free time, I like to spend it
   a) touching up my hair color.
   b) reading a good book.
   c) being mean to less popular people.

2. My favorite activity is
   a) hugging people.
   b) creating art/crafts.
   c) shopping.

3. My past relationships with guys can best be described as
   a) short and sweet and numerous.
   b) practically nonexistent.
   c) a steady BF for months or years.

4. The main things I look for in a guy are
   a) that he's a guy. (I'm not picky.)
   b) brains and a sense of humor.
   c) looks and threads.

5. At lunch, I am most likely to sit with
   a) my crush.
   b) my BFF.
   c) the popular crowd.

6. My friends describe me as
   a) unusual.
   b) a good student.
   c) pretty.

7. When I have time to read, I
   a) take a nap or text instead.
   b) pick up a novel.
   c) buy a magazine.

8. People who don't know me well might describe me as
   a) mysterious.
   b) shy.
   c) beautiful.

9. My dream date would be
   a) any date.
   b) a carriage ride and putt-putt.
   c) a HS football game and post-game party.

10. Right now, the desk/dresser in my room probably has
    a) a bottle of black nail polish on it.
    b) half-finished projects scattered about.
    c) a cool laptop with Faceplace on the screen.

START

Would you rather play a game (sports or video) with friends or go on a date?

GAME

DATE

Do you like to read?

YE

TALK

NO

Would you prefer to talk quietly or go somewhere loud where you can be seen?

Would you like to spend time looking at art or looking in a mirror?

ART

MIRR

SEEN!

NO!

Do you care if your date is considered beautiful by others?

YES!

Bedtime

Got permission from Mom to make sixty-three copies of my girl survey and fifty-two copies of the boy one. I'm ready to put my project into action tomorrow!

Did not get to sit with Evan at lunch. ☹ But I passed him twice in the hall and he smiled both times! ☺ ☺ Ahhhhh—progress!

Tuesday, January 9
Fourth period

I just distributed my surveys. (Mr. DeLacey said he'd take his later.) In my head I pictured the three letter-shaped boxes on the boys' survey as three different girls: The Vine (type

A), me (type B), and Maybelline (type C). I hope, hope, hope that lots of guys will follow the path that leads to Type B—me!

I'm sure most scientists would frown on it, but the boys' survey won't *exactly* be anonymous. Well, it was for *most* of Mr. DeLacey's math classes, but not for fourth period (the class I'm in).

That's because we always sit in the same seats in his class. So before handing them out, I *very lightly* (and very tinily) wrote a code number on the back of each sheet. I used the old initials-are-assigned-a-number-based-on-their-place-in-the-alphabet code. (The code for my initials is 11-13, for example.)

This way, I'll be sure to know if there's anyone in my class who's likely to be a match for me. Perfect!

Bedtime

Even though I was able to distribute my surveys today, it was not the greatest day because

1. I didn't get to sit with Evan at lunch. Again.
2. I heard Maybelline talking about how stupid my surveys were. And even though I don't care what she thinks at all, I really do.

3. Maybelline thwarted my research during fifth period! She asked what my note cards were for when I pulled them out of my backpack, so I had *no choice* but to stuff them back in. I'm going to have to keep an eye on her if I want to continue my observations. This is a huge problem since she sits *behind* me, and last time I checked, "eyes in the back of the head" is a genetic mutation currently unavailable to humans.

Wednesday, January 10
Sixth period

Maybe I'm just being paranoid, but I felt the hawk eyes beneath Maybelline's pale green eyelids on me *all day*. Band is the one class I don't have with her, so this is the first time I've been brave enough to do a little more research. (We're supposed to be "warming up.") Since I only have two classes with Malcolm Maxwell, and this is one of them, I might as well concentrate on him.

Data Collected on: 1/10   Status: Available
Hair: Brown hang-bang
Eyes: Barely visible due to hang-bang
Eyebrows: Invisible due to hang-bang
Body Type: Bony
Age: 13
Nice-o-meter: ☺☺☺
Interest Level: ♥♥♥
Fast Fact: Loves to skateboard

Malcolm is a quiet guy. I'd say his soul, like his eyes, is partially hidden (in a not-unattractive, mysterious way). He's cool without being conceited, somehow. Unfortunately, I can't observe him too much since the drums are at the back of the class — two rows behind the trumpets.

He's not the type of guy that you just go up to and start a conversation with. It would be too odd. Or too obvious. Or something. But once we bumped into each other when he was coming out of the instrument room. I immediately glanced down. (Why don't I have the guts to look cute, mysterious guys in the eyes?) This gave me a chance to check out those doodles he puts on his high-tops.

He's a good artist! I mumbled that I liked his Chucks. And he said, "Cool." And now you know one hundred percent of the words we've exchanged. Ever.

Mr. Waldorf is rapping his baton on the podium. Gotta go!

After dinner

Tonight I got a phone call. One that *ruined my life.* One that started with Tabbi saying: "Do you think Evan Carlson is cute?"

I did.

"Don't you think he's nice, too?"

I did.

"Do you think he'd make a good boyfriend?"

Did I!

I closed my eyes and crossed my fingers. This had to be it. Evan had talked to Tabbi and told her that he liked me!

But that is not what happened. Not at all.

"I'm so glad you think so, Kara! I want my best friend and my boyfriend to get along." Tabbi giggled.

I stopped breathing.

"Anna told me that Evan is going to ask me to go out! Wanna guess what I'm going to say?"

I didn't.

"I'm going to say yes! I'll finally have a boyfriend! Do you believe it?"

I didn't.

"As of this time tomorrow, I, Tabbi Reddy, will have a boyfriend."

But I didn't.

Tabbi kept talking. "That doesn't mean I don't want you to still hang out with me and Evan. If you hadn't gotten me to go talk to him at lunch, he might not have ever noticed me!"

Thank you, tightwad parents, for denying my request for a webcam! My eyes were overflowing and my heart was thumping so wildly that I'm sure Tabs would have seen it trying to burst through my sweater. Plus, I know my burning face must have been the color of my tom-tom heart.

Do you have any idea how hard it is to pretend to be happy for your best friend when *she* is the reason your heart is breaking? It's the hardest thing I've ever done — even harder than the time I got stuck having to help my eighty-seven-year-old great-grandma fasten her bra, which has, like, fifteen hooks. And it's really hard to fasten them, by the way, when you're closing your eyes and trying to imagine that you are somewhere — anywhere — else.

But I had to pretend to be happy even though what I really wanted to do was call her a boy stealing FBF (*F*ormer *B*est *F*riend, not to be confused with BFF). I wanted to hate her. But I couldn't. Tabbi had no idea that I liked Evan, and telling her now would only make her feel bad. Plus, it wouldn't change anything. He still liked her . . . not me.

Why hadn't I told her how I felt about Evan during one of those LONG conversations when she was blabbing about Alex? WHY? WHY? WHY? Tabs wouldn't have looked twice at Evan if she knew I liked him.

I will be the Spinster of Spring Valley Middle School. I'll be voted Most Likely To Die Alone. I'll be the eternal bachelorette, without an entourage of good-looking guys rounded up by television producers for me to pick from.

Tabs talked on and on about how great Evan is. She didn't seem to notice that I wasn't talking. It gave me a chance to compose myself, but shouldn't she have noticed that her BFF was silent? Yes! She should have! I finally found my voice enough to ask if she was *sure* she didn't still like Alex. I wish I hadn't because she said, "I thought I did. But Alex was just an illusion of love. Evan is the real thing. I don't think I'm really Alex's type. I was wasting my time."

Great. *Now* she figures this out. I didn't know whether to scream or puke. I think if you do both at the same time, your head might explode or something. I might give it a shot though. At the moment, I'd prefer an exploding head to an exploding heart.

Thursday, January 11
First period

When I got to school, Tabbi and Evan were all pretzeled together, before the first bell even rang. I'm going to try to go home sick.

Third period

Mrs. Hill said I didn't look sick to her. I had to go back to my seat.

Lunch

Spending whole lunch period in library to avoid cafeteria! Yesterday it would've thrilled me to sit near Evan. Not today.

Only guy in the library is Jonah Nate Stewart. He has a big stack of Civil War books spread out on a table. Last year it'd have been Revolutionary War books. His dad's a captain in the Marines, which explains his haircut and love of war books but not his body.

He's here. I'm here. So here it goes—even though the thought that I might end up with someone like Jonah Nate is depressing.

Subject Number #9: JONAH NATE STEWART
Data Collected on: 1/11   Status: Should be obvious
Hair: High and tight
Eyes: Huge. Magnified by thick glasses
Eyebrows: Hidden. Concealed by rims of thick glasses
Body Type: Chubby
Age: 12
Nice-o-meter: ☺☺
Interest Level: 0!
Fast Fact: Loves moldy old wars and thinks other people do, too

Oh no. Jonah Nate just caught my eye and is motioning for me to come look at something. This could be worse than watching Evan and Tabbi at lunch.

Ten minutes later (Seemed like an hour)

Before I even reached Jonah Nate's table, he was spouting facts from the book he was waving in his hand. "Hey, Kara, did you know that the *Hunley* was the first successful combat submarine?" he loud-whispered, even though there was no one else around. "And it was powered by men? And that it sank off the coast of Charleston, South Carolina, with all eight crew members still on board?"

I shook my head, pulled a book from the shelf, and tried to look absorbed by page 72. Jonah Nate didn't take the hint.

"And one of the men, Lieutenant Dixon, carried a lucky gold coin that had saved his life in the Battle of Shiloh? The coin was given to him by his sweetheart. You could still read the words he'd carved into it when they recovered it from the *Hunley* over a hundred years later!"

That got my attention. Was the powerful golden coin a gift from Dixon's soul mate? I pointed to the book clutched in his hand and asked if the information about Lieutenant Dixon was in it.

"Yeah!" said Jonah Nate enthusiastically.

I asked if I could borrow the book.

Jonah Nate didn't look so enthusiastic anymore. "I don't know. . . . It's from my personal collection."

I figured any reading I could do about soul mates is going to help my research, so I promised to return his precious book the very next day if he'd let me borrow it. (As if I'd really keep a book about the Civil War lying around.)

So here I sit with a book about the *Hunley*, hoping to find Lieutenant Dixon's name in the index so I can just go straight to the pages about him. I don't have time to read the whole darn thing. And really, who'd want to? Besides Jonah Nate, I mean.

Fifth period

Evan has something written all over his hand. In Tabbi's handwriting. I'm trying to read it. Even though I don't care what she wrote at all, I really do.

There, he's raising his hand to give an answer for the question that Ms. Sabatino just asked: "What do you call the force that occurs when one object rubs against another?"

Evan said, "Friction." His hand said *Property of Tabbi Reddy*. Blech.

Ms. Sabatino said Evan was right. I say it depends on what the objects are. If one object is Evan Carlson, and the other object is Tabbi Reddy, I'm pretty sure the answer is *disgusting* or *betrayal* or something.

If you saw me right now, Mrs. Hill, I'm pretty sure you'd say I look sick!

Bedtime (According to my parents. For once I think they're right.)

Phone is ringing. I know without looking at caller ID that it's Tabbi. There's no way she'd miss calling me today. It's what a best friend does when she has a new boyfriend.

Tabs: Where were you at lunch? Evan and I looked for you.

Me: Oh. Well. I decided to go to the library.

Tabs: The library! The only person who hangs out there during lunch is Jonah Nate.

Me: (*Don't I know it.*) Well, I had to do some research.

Tabs: For what?

Me: (*Saying the first thing that pops into my head*) Science fair.

Tabs: I thought those surveys we took were your project.

Me: They are, but . . .

Tabs: Hey! Will you be able to let me know if Evan and I turn out to be compatible?

Me: (*Crossing my fingers*) No. It was a blind study.

Tabs: Oh.

Me: I've gotta go.

Tabs: Wait! I need to tell you something.

Me: Hmmm?

Tabs: Thanks.

Me: For what?

Tabs: For leading me to Evan's table. And for getting detention. (*She actually giggled!*) The day I went and sat by him by myself was the day Evan realized he liked me.

Me: Glad I could help. Can we talk later? I've felt sick all day and I feel even worse now.

Tabs: (*Sounding confused*) Feel better, then. . . .

Me: Bye.

I didn't lie to Tabbi. I really did feel sick when I hung up the phone. Even sicker than before, because something was suddenly clear to me. That stupid prank I pulled with Chip had cost me my crush.

Friday, January 12
Lunch

Today promises to be just as bad as yesterday. Tabbi wrote the same dumb words on Evan's hand. Again. I couldn't face lunch with them. Again. So here I am in the library. Again. Actually, I *had* to come here because Jonah Nate's not letting me forget my promise. Every time he saw me this morning, he said, "Do you have my book, Kara? You *promised.*" Unfortunately, he seems to reserve his loud-whispering for the library.

The last time he cornered me about the dreaded book, we were in the hallway right in front of Maybelline and The Sponge.

Maybelline said, "What book, Kara? *How to Be Popular in Ten Easy Steps?*"

Unfortunately, Jonah Nate is deaf to sarcasm. "No!" he yelled. "A book about a Civil War submarine!"

This made it worse, not better, because Maybelline and The Sponge grabbed each other and giggled. "Keep reading books like that, Kara. That'll improve your social life," sputtered Maybelline.

"Except that she doesn't have one," added The Sponge.

Then they walked off holding each other up. Apparently, my borrowing a book from Jonah Nate is the funniest thing either of them has ever heard.

It's okay to be furious with someone for saying something that's basically true, isn't it?

I took my anger out on Jonah Nate. "You'll have your precious book by the end of lunch. Do NOT ask me about it again!"

So. I'm poring over this book, wishing I'd just gone ahead and read it last night. But last night I kept finding better things to do. Like creating a bead, button, and fishing line curtain to hang across the door of my room. I really got into making it, probably because whenever I'm concentrating on transforming something boring (like fishing line) into something amazing (like a beaded curtain), my problems (like Tabbi and Evan) seem far, far away.

I guess every girl needs some way to escape her problems. Julie runs from hers. I mean, she runs every morning no matter what. But I've noticed that she also goes running if she's just had an argument with Mom or something.

She's lucky that she's picked a way to escape that actually does her some good! All of those hours escaping have netted her a MVP award and a bunch of shiny track trophies.

Unfortunately for me, you don't win room-enhancing trophies by escaping into a good book or a craft project. On the other hand, the beaded curtain is technically room-enhancing. Plus, getting away from the idea of Tabbi and Evan for a few hours was great. But now it's back to reality. And reality wants his precious book back. Better get to reading.

Ten minutes later . . .

Okay, I just finished reading all about Lieutenant Dixon and his soul mate, Queenie Bennett. I know Lieutenant Dixon is dead. But if he weren't, here's what his information would look like:

Subject Number #10: LIEUTENANT GEORGE DIXON
Data Collected on: 1/12   Status: DOA
Hair: Sandy blond. Mustache
Eyes: ?
Eyebrows: ?
Body Type: Athletic
Age: 28 forever
Fast Fact: Token from his soul mate was with him when he died.

Even though researching a dead person in the stillness of the library is creeping me out a little bit, this stuff has raised some serious questions that need to be included in my research.

Question 1: What if the person destined to be your one and only true soul mate dies before you have a chance to get married?

Queenie Bennett and Lieutenant George Dixon were destined for each other! The gold coin she gave him acted like a powerful mini shield when it was in his pocket. It stopped a bullet! Clearly, the coin was protected by Queenie's love.

Over a hundred years later—when they pulled the *Hunley* out of Charleston Harbor—that gold coin was still next to Dixon's body. If that's not true love, I don't know what is.

Question 2: Can a person have more than one soul mate?

Seven years after Dixon died, his true love married someone else! What if the question "Who is my one and only soul mate?" has a multiple-choice answer . . . and more than one answer is correct?

Question 3: What if the universe got out of whack and your one and only true soul mate was Lieutenant Dixon or some other person from a century or so ago and you NEVER even had the chance to find him?

It makes my head hurt to think about it. I mean, there are so many more possibilities for finding your soul mate if life works like it does in *Prada and Prejudice*, which is a book about a girl who stumbles into nineteenth-century England and then falls in love with someone there. It's hard enough trying to find potential soul mates among my current class-mates, never mind the entire world population, past and present. I'm giving Jonah Nate his book back right now!

Sixth period

Tabbi asked me if I wanted to walk to Burger King with her and Evan after school to get a milk shake. I didn't.

Saturday, January 13
After dinner

There's nothing like a little trip to the mall to lift a girl's spirits, even if the goal of the trip is to get new running shoes for her sister the track star. Because guess what else there is at the mall besides impact-resistant shoes with flexible cushioning?

Cute guys that you can't see at your school! Cute guys who could possibly be your soul mate! Hey—you never know. I took notes on one who works at A&F.

See, I was in there checking out tops while Julie was trying on shoes. Suddenly, I felt this hand on my arm.

I turned around and the guy of my dreams was saying, "Can I help you?"

I wanted to say, "Yes, you can!" But instead I mumbled that I was just looking, and hurried out of the store because I could feel my face turning red. But I felt something else, too—an all-over tingle—especially when he touched my arm. What if that's a feeling that *only* your one and only true soul mate can give you?

Subject Number #11: GUY AT THE MALL
AKA Justin (according to his plastic name tag)
Data Collected on: 1/13   Status: ?
Hair: Straight and blond. Sideburns!
Eyes: Greenish, gorgeous
Eyebrows: Perfectly arched. Perfectly thick
Body Type: Wow
Age: 16ish
Nice-o-meter: ☺☺☺☺☺
Interest Level: ♥ ♥ ♥ ♥ ♥
Question: When the skin on your arm tingles where a guy who looks like this touched it, is it a sign that he's your soul mate?

Sunday, January 14
After lunch

Bebe Truelove dished out another helping of worthless advice today along with an ad for breath spray. Here's the e-mail I just received:

To: Kara M <Craftychick@mailquickly.com>
From: BebeTruelove <bebe@bebetruelove.com>
Subject: Tip #2

Dear Soul Mate Seeker,

A guy likes a girl who listens to him when he talks. When having conversations, remember that your ears are just as important as your mouth.

Tip #2: Be a good listener.

Good Luck in Love,
Bebe

See why I think this advice is worthless? When I dragged Tabbi over to Evan's table, I hardly talked at all. I was an excellent listener! I listened to Evan. I listened to Tabbi. I listened to Tabbi talk to Evan. And look what it got me. A front-row seat at the *Best Friend Steals Crush* show.

WEEK 2: RESEARCH REVIEW
# of subjects unobtrusively observed: 5

Findings: All subjects this week are single (as far as I know). I think there is potential in Subject #8, and maybe Subject #11, and – in 10 years or so – Subject #7.
Most significant finding:
Keep BFF away from potential BF!

Bebe Truelove's Tip #2:
Be a good listener. Blah. Blah. Blah.

Data Collection Methods: observation, magazines

Tuesday, January 16
Fourth period

So Mr. DeLacey has a sub today. Chip caught my arm as I was coming in the door. (It didn't create an all-over tingle.)

"Operation Class-List Swap?" he suggested. He wiggled his mediocre eyebrows. I couldn't help laughing.

But I wasn't sure it was a good idea. After all, the last time I participated in one of his pranks, it cost me these things:

1. the guy of my dreams.
2. the ability to tolerate my best friend's conversations.
3. my chance for total happiness.

Right. I really had nothing left to lose. I gave Chip the thumbs-up.

He sat in the last seat of the last row so he could be the one to switch the list out before carrying it up to the sub. We'd started with normal-looking names like Candace B. Fureal. Moved on to Marcus Absent (totally appropriate) and ended with our joint favorite: Monk E. Butts. (Okay, there were some better ones, but we *knew* we'd get in trouble for using those.)

I pretended to be getting something out of my desk when Chip walked up to the front to turn in the list so that no one would notice me trying not to laugh. Nobody did. When I thought about how successful I was at going unnoticed, it was kind of depressing. . . .

After school

At the beginning of sixth period, Tabbi left the woodwind section during warm-ups to come sit with me in brass. We often use this time to catch up because no one can hear what we're saying with the horns tooting, drums banging, and woodwinds squeaking all at once. Anyway, Tabs wanted to know what was wrong. I've been trying to act normal around her, but it's hard. Knowing it's not her fault that Evan likes her instead of me somehow doesn't help.

I can't even blame him for that. There's a lot to like about Tabbi! She's loyal. And she always gives straight-up answers for whatever questions you ask. She has great hair. It's thick and blond, but she has the confidence to wear it short. I guess Evan sees these great things, too.

But why couldn't he see all the great things about *me*? Like how I make almost all A's. I mean, I could be the money-earner and he could live a life of leisure as my soul mate! He'll never get that with Tabbi. Trust me.

And how I'm good at creating things. I mean, not many people have the imagination to turn an Altoids tin into a mini suitcase with masking tape, shoe polish, and a piece of wire. And I love to laugh! I'd laugh at all of his crazy comments and stupid jokes. Why couldn't Evan have seen this? Why? Why? Why?

I decided to tell Tabbi the truth. But not all of it. I told her it was hard for me to not have a boyfriend, especially now that she did.

"One day the right guy is going to see how great you are." Tabbi hugged me. And I appreciated it. But I wish we'd been paying more attention to the podium. Because Mr. Waldorf stepped up and everyone fell silent and put down their instruments just as Tabbi added, "Don't worry, Kara, you'll get a boyfriend soon."

Bus ride home

"I'm *sorry!*" Tabbi said as I climbed up the metal steps and through the folding door.

I couldn't answer her. I knew I'd cry, and I was humiliated enough already.

By this time tomorrow the whole school will know that I want a boyfriend. I'll look desperate. And okay, I am desperate. But does *everybody* have to know?

The minute I got home

As soon as I stepped off of the bus, my cell rang. It was Maybelline! That girl has rotten timing.

"Hey, Kara. This is Colleen. I heard you left school upset

and I just wanted to know what's wrong. All those A's not helping you get a boyfriend?"

Click.

After dinner

After Maybelline's call, I went straight to Mom's craft corner, which is down in the basement along with our old sofa, old TV, and old everything else. You know, stuff that isn't good enough to keep upstairs but is too good to throw away. I felt like breaking something, and there's a lot of old junk stashed with the craft supplies. I grabbed a loop of wire and twisted it, twisted it, twisted it until it looked like an angry blob. But the blob also kinda looked like a fish. So I added fins and threaded a blue bead on for an eye.

In the end, the fish looked really cool! And you know what? I felt a lot better. Mom always says that creating is a form of healing. I think she's right!

angry blob

cute pin

Bedtime. For real.

Just got a text from Tabbi.

Plz 4giv me.

She's probably afraid to call. I'm glad. I don't want to talk to her. But I do forgive her.

So just before I turned out the lights, after I knew her mom had taken her phone away (she's waaay strict about bedtime), I texted Tabbi back.

OK

Wednesday, January 17
First period

Evan smiled at me when he passed by just now. At one point I would have thought this was a great sign, but now I do not.

Lunch

Whew. Everyone seems to have forgotten about what Tabbi said in band, probably because there's bigger news. Phillip Bernard (of gorgeous eyebrow fame) got—and then lost—his first official girlfriend last night.

Phillip is really cute, but he's also so shy that he's never actually gone out with anyone. We've all been wondering who he liked. Apparently, he texted Elizabeth R and asked her to go out. Then ten minutes after she said yes, he changed his mind and broke it off. With another text. Yep, they got together and broke up without seeing each other OR actually talking. Now she *hates* him, supposedly. I hope she wasn't supposed to be his one and only soul mate!

After school

Well. I've certainly gathered more information on Mr. DeLacey than I ever wanted to know. I know so much about him now that I need to scrap my first index card and make a new one.

Subject #7: Mr. DELACEY (Card 2)
Data Collected on: 1/17   Status: Too old!
Hair: Same as before
Eyes: Ditto
Eyebrows: Ditto
Body Type: Too old
Age: Too old
Nice-o-meter: ☹
Interest Level: 0
Fast Fact: No sense of humor. At all!

Apparently, replacing real names with funny fake names is not equally funny to all people. At first I figured Mr. DeLacey wasn't too upset about our prank because he acted completely normal during algebra. But after class he handed me a note that I was momentarily, I admit, just a bit excited about taking. Then I opened it.

Come to my room after school
for detention.
I've already contacted your parents.
They'll pick you up thirty minutes late.

By the time I got to science, the note had gotten damp in my nervous, sweaty hands. But I felt a little better when I saw Chip smiling and waving his little white note like a flag of surrender. We'd underestimated what an important fueling station the teacher's lounge is on the information highway. Mrs. Hill squealed on us!

Somehow I could tell detention wasn't going to be as much fun this time. I think that's because Mr. DeLacey used the phrase "contacted your parents" in his note, and one thing's for sure: Nothing is as much fun when your parents are involved.

Later, in detention, I learned that in addition to being good at explaining math, Mr. DeLacey can also really deliver a lecture. And not the fun kind like *Why gummy worms grow three times their size when soaked in water.* The kind you usually hear coming out of a parent's mouth. He started with what a hard job substitutes have, got louder when he asked if we knew how difficult it is to get a sub when kids don't behave, and then veered into how extremely rude and disrespectful we were to force someone to read crude names like Monk E. Butts! (Good thing he didn't know about the names that *didn't* make the list.)

He ended the lecture with "Do you get it now?" (Let me tell you, that phrase is *never* going to mean the same thing to me in algebra.) I just nodded my head and knew that I was going to have to do a lot of explaining to my mom when we got home.

And I knew something else, too. I'd never look into those big blue eyes again and think they're really nice. But the experience did teach me something:

Don't try to pull one over on a math teacher. They're too good at figuring things out.

Bedtime

Mom made me hand over my cell phone as soon as we got in the car. She said instead of talking to my friends, I should be thinking about the fact that "misbehaving for a substitute is actually disrespecting the regular teacher." I guess when she came to pick me up she saw what I used to see in Mr.

DeLacey's big blue eyes while he explained how Chip and I had "violated the teacher-student bonds of trust." All I know is she sure was nodding a lot while he talked to her. He was probably hoping she'd lay an additional punishment on me, too. She did. Kind of. She de-phoned me.

I don't really mind this punishment because I'm pretty sure it just saved the life of my cell phone. I swear I'm going to throw it in the toilet if Tabbi calls me one more time to tell me that Evan Carlson is perfect and that she is absolutely positively in love. She thinks it's "the real thing." They have now been together for the six longest days of my life.

I don't want to think about it. Instead, I'll think about the fact that a ton of middle-school romances last less than a week. So there's a pretty good chance that one day they'll break up. Maybe tomorrow, even. Then I'll still have a chance with Evan. Because, you know, you never know. . . .

Thursday, January 18
Fourth period

Dear Mr. DeLacey,

I know what you're doing even though I'm not looking at you. I try to avoid looking at you now because I've realized your soul is mean. And somehow seeing the mean side of a person's soul changes the way his face looks, too. That's right. The number of girls in our class who think you are cute has just been reduced by one. You do the math!

I know what you're doing because you do the same exact things every day. I can hear the *drrrrrrrrr* of your right-hand desk drawer, so I know you're putting away your thermal lunch bag. Now I hear steps. You're walking to the file cabinet to get out lesson plans. You just walked back across the room and stopped, which means you're placing them in the middle of your very clean desk. *Click!* The top drawer of your desk has just closed, which means you've pulled out a green ballpoint pen and are scribbling a green circle on the note cube on your desk.

In my eyes you've changed, Mr. DeLacey, but you're still following the same old routine. And now that I'm not watching you follow it anymore, I have time to do other things. Like describe how torturous lunch period has become. See, Tabbi is determined to prove her loyalty to me by making sure I still sit with her even though she's sitting with the guy I secretly like. It is more torturous than afternoon detention with you. More torturous than having to eat Mimi's asparagus soup "or else," and *that's* something I have to choke down one tiny little mouthful at a time. Not that you care about love and relationships and how painful it is to have your best friend drooling over your crush while all you have to drool over is your PB&J. If you cared about stuff like that you'd probably be married by now. And you'd be nicer.

When I'm with Tabs and Evan, my only option is to focus on something else. Unfortunately, there aren't many great things to look at in the cafeteria. Today I observed The Vine and James sneaking a kiss when the teacher on duty was writing up a kid for dumping food on his friend. Mashed potatoes look bad enough when they're served in a section of green plastic tray. They look even worse when they're served on a bed of human hair. Yet even *that* sight is more appetizing than The Vine and James intertwined. (Asparagus soup is more appetizing than that!) So I looked away and spotted Richie.

I haven't done any unobtrusive observations of Richie yet, so I watched him for a while.

He always smiles! (Maybe if you took a moment to study him, some of that smiling would rub off on you.) Richie smiles when he knows the answers in class. He smiles when he doesn't. He's been smiling since he moved here, but he doesn't talk much.

It's hard to image how Richie could possibly be my one and only true soul mate, because we don't hang out in the same group at all and we've never really talked. But I need to include him in my research. Because, like I always say . . . you never know.

I'm still not looking at you, Mr. DeLacey, but I can tell you're ready to start class because you're tapping that green pen against your palm. Time to pull out the algebra homework.

Signed, but never to be delivered by,

Kara McAllister

P.S. You can give me those surveys for my science fair project any time now.

Subject #12: RICHIE LOPEZ
Data Collected on: 1/18   Status: Single
Hair: Black. Straight
Eyes: Brown
Eyebrows: Arched
Body Type: Average
Age: 12
Nice-o-meter: ☺☺☺☺☺
Interest Level: ♥
Fast Fact: Bilingual

Sixth period

We have a sub in band, which is great because most subs don't know anything about waving a baton. (Heck, most *people* don't know anything about waving a baton.) So we're basically having study hall in the band room. I've been trying to concentrate on solving for x, but thinking about algebra makes me think about Mr. DeLacey, which makes me think about my science project surveys, which makes me think about the fact that Mr. DeLacey hasn't given them back to me, which makes me think about how I'm afraid to ask for them since he was so angry about the funny fake-name list and all. But the clock is ticking (< three weeks until the due date) and I *need* to get them in time to create a chart and a science board. I'll ask for them right after school. I won't be afraid. I won't be afraid. . . .

Bus ride home

So after school, I asked Mr. DeLacey in my *sweetest possible* voice if he'd had time to distribute my surveys.

He said, "Yes, Kara, I took your little 'survey.'" When he said "survey," he used air quotes. I hate air quotes. Nothing good ever happens between air quotes.

"Can you give them back to me so I can finish my project?" I asked.

Mr. DeLacey turned his back to me and acted like he was straightening his desk, but come on, he has the neatest desk you've ever seen. It probably qualifies as a sterile environment. Like, surgery could be performed on that desk. "No," he said to his desk.

I didn't think I'd heard him right. "When can I get them?" I asked.

"Kara, you need to accept the fact that there's nothing

scientific about those surveys. Take my advice and come up with a new project. You'll thank me when you get a grade higher than an F."

At that point, I was glad Mr. DeLacey had his back to me because water was pooling in my eyes. I couldn't tell whether anger or embarrassment caused this reaction. See, I don't think Mr. DeLacey was acting purely in my best interests to help me make a better science grade. I think he was being a jerk because he could be. Because he is a teacher and I am not, and he is mad that I embarrassed him in front of the substitute. Or maybe he's just a mean person who's only nice if you do everything one-hundred-percent exactly right. Maybe that's why he's still single. I don't know. Do mean people get to have soul mates?

After dinner

Mom and Dad always want us to tell them about our day when we have family dinners, which my mom likes to think happens every night. Actually, we only all manage to make it around the table three or four nights a week. Of course the number of nights I'm present, unfortunately, is something close to . . . I'd say . . . every single night. But Julie is so busy with track and her fabulous social life that she doesn't frequent the McAllister Café as often as I do. Lucky me.

Tonight, though, I was looking forward to the discussion because I wanted to get my dad's take on Mr. DeLacey and my STOLEN surveys. Even if I can't use them for a science fair project, they contain *valuable* information—especially if they prove my Hidden Agenda Soul Mate Project Hypothesis correct! I need them! And I figured my dad would know how I could get them back.

Dad is an attorney. But he's not the kind of attorney that makes a lot of money. See, he works for a human rights organization, and humanity is not a very valuable commodity compared to something like real estate. But why is humanity more important than his own flesh and blood? Well, at least he still gives me useful advice. Sometimes.

As soon as we started passing the food, I told the Evil DeLacey Survey Stealer story.

Julie said, "Mr. DeLacey? Isn't that the teacher you think is so cute?"

Thanks, Julie. I *so* appreciate your contribution to getting Mom and Dad to take my conversation seriously. And why'd you have to be home for dinner tonight of all nights?

But luckily, Dad had his advice ready and he started giving it before I was forced to answer Julie's dumb question. Not that she really needed the answer. She knew it before she asked.

Anyway, Dad said, "You get the answers you want if you ask the right questions."

I gave him the usual response. "Huh?"

"Just walk up to Mr. DeLacey and politely ask, 'Is it legal for you to keep my surveys, which are my property, if I ask you for them back?'"

"You really think I have the guts to do that?"

"Depends on how bad you want the surveys."

I want them bad. Tune in tomorrow to see if it's bad enough. . . .

Friday, January 19
Sixth period

I now have the surveys in my hands and the memory of the look in Mr. DeLacey's burning ice-blue eyes (after I asked the "Is it legal?" question) seared into my brain. I sure hope he doesn't know how to make voodoo dolls or anything.

After school

Tabbi asked if I wanted to go out to eat pizza and go to a movie with her and Evan. Um . . . NO! I'd rather eat asparagus soup at Mimi's. Besides, I really want to finish compiling my surveys. I'm done with the girls' one. The results turned out a little differently than I expected.

I thought that most of the girls would have circled at least eight or nine of the same letter, so that they would clearly fall into one group or the other. But that's not what happened at all. A lot of girls picked almost even combinations of letters, like four As, three Bs, and three Cs. When that happened, I would put them in whatever group they had most of, but it made me wonder: Is a girl really Type A if she only picks four A answers? Maybe my test needed to have more questions.

Out of sixty-three girls, here is the number of girls in each type:

Type A: 22
Type B: 13
Type C: 28

By the way, almost *no one* thinks their friends describe them as unusual (think again, girls!) and almost *everyone* has a cool laptop on their desk at home. Right.

Late. Too late. So late it's almost early. Too early.

Well, I compiled the results of the boys' survey. Then I did it again to make sure I'd calculated right the first time. Unfortunately, I had. Mr. D may be a jerk, but he has to be right about one thing. This "survey" (imagine air quotes around preceding word) cannot possibly be scientifically accurate! No way! Because here are what the results look like:

No! No! No! A Googol Times No: The Results of My Stinking Survey by Kara McAllister

Which Type Do Guys Like?

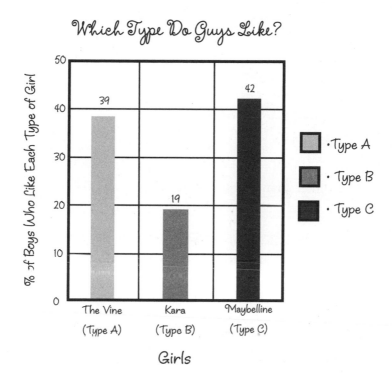

Girls

Source: my stupid surveys

And that's not even the bad news! The bad news is that of the subjects who were secretly identified using my seating chart + number-for-initials code, here are the ones who liked Type B girls: Jonah Nate, Alex Langford, and Mr. D (I know because it was the only one in green ink). Only three! Since I've already ruled all three of those guys out as potential soul mates, this survey is just as worthless to my soul mate project as it is to my science fair project. Ugh! Now I have to come up with a totally new idea!

Saturday, January 20
Afternoon

At least this week's advice from Bebe gave me something to do for a change. Here is her latest e-mail:

To: Kara M <Craftychick@mailquickly.com>
From: BebeTruelove <bebe@bebetruelove.com>
Subject: Tip #3

Dear Soul Mate Seeker,

Know what you want! Think about the qualities you would like to find in a soul mate. Now make a list. Once you know what you are looking for, it will be easier to find.

Tip #3: Know what you want!

Good Luck in Love,

Bebe

Okay, Bebe. I can handle that one!

The Perfect Soul Mate: A List
by Kara McAllister

My one and only soul mate will

1. be a nice person.
2. have a sense of humor.
3. like to read.
4. appreciate art.
5. think I'm great.

Well, that's all I have so far. But that's only because I don't know enough about kissing or anything to have added "be a good kisser" for number 6.

Sunday, January 21
Bedtime

Until around 3:30 this afternoon, there was only one word I could use to describe my weekend: *depressing*!

My survey results were disastrous. My best friend is with the only guy I liked. And judging by the height-challenged middle column in the chart I made, I, Kara McAllister, am apparently the least attractive type of girl possible to the opposite sex.

Then I remembered something that gave me hope. I call him Subject #11. That's right. Guy at the Mall. He, at least, has not taken my survey! Maybe he's mature enough to like girls like me: Type B!

Once I remembered this detail, I had to find a way to get back to the mall. And I could only think of one sure-fire way: Tell Mom I was taking up running so I'd need a pair of track shoes. I knew Mom would have a very hard time turning down my request because she's obsessed with not showing favoritism between Julie and me. And yes, I do use this information to my advantage sometimes because I think Julie already has most of the advantages. It's only fair. Besides, information isn't worth having if you don't use it.

So I walked into the family room and said, "I want to try out for track this year."

Mom, Dad, and Julie looked at me. But apparently an evil

fairy had just visited the room and blasted my family with a spell that rendered (new vocab word) each of them mute. No one said a single word.

Ignoring the possible presence of a malevolent (new vocab word) fairy, I forged ahead. "Track has been such a great experience for Julie. And I really need to do something to get more involved with school."

Silence.

"Can you take me to the mall so I can get some track shoes like you got Julie?"

Family still mute.

"I promise to start running with Julie every morning."

"What?!" yelled Julie. "You've never been interested in track!"

I guess I was wrong about the voice-stealing fairy.

"But I'm older now," I said. "You had a chance to prove yourself in track. I should too."

Julie, now mute again, rolled her eyes.

Mom sighed. "Are you sure track is your thing, Kara?"

"You never even go jogging," added Dad.

"You guys are always saying I should try new things." (When the going gets tough, use your parents' own words against them.)

"Why don't we go to Michaels and get some new craft supplies instead?" asked Mom.

"Because craft supplies can't buy you love," I said.

Julie made a sound that resembled a raft deflating. "And track shoes can?"

"They seem to be working for you."

Julie's face turned pink, for some reason. She tossed her ponytail and stomped from the room. What's up with her?

In the end, Mom took me to the mall like I knew she would. Unfortunately, however, my mom doesn't believe in "dropping young girls off at the mall by themselves." So she was totally unreasonable and insisted on coming along.

And since I wasn't about to drag Mom into A&F, I only had about fifty seconds to dash in there while she was looking at half-price baking dishes. Guess what. No Justin. I asked the salesclerk if he was working today and she said, "How do you know Justin?" (As if it's any of her business!!!!)

Then two things happened at the exact wrong time. Justin walked in from the back of the store (he looked even better than before, if that's possible), and my mom showed up at the front. I ran out, pulling her toward the food court. But I heard the clerk say, "Do you know that girl? She was looking for you."

"Who, *her*?" he asked. He used a tone that means "NO!" in about eighty-two different languages.

What a narrowly avoided disaster! But do I think there's still a chance he could be my soul mate? Sure! Because you never know. . . .

# of subjects unobtrusively observed: 2

Most significant finding: People who seem perfectly nice are actually jerks, sometimes.

New Research Strategy: Field trip to the mall

Bebe Truelove's Tip #3: Know what you want.

Data Collection Methods: observation, surveys

Monday, January 22
7:00 a.m.

Usually I'm just rolling out of bed at this time in the morning. But not today. That's because today's the first day I had to *pretend* to want to go running with Julie since I made Mom buy me those shoes. So at 6:00 this morning Julie shook me awake, not too gently either. "Mom says I *have* to take you running. Thanks. I'm leaving in five — with or without you."

The last thing I wanted to do at 6:00 a.m. was to go running with my resentful sister (especially since I'm no closer to knowing if Justin is my one and only soul mate), but I knew if I didn't make a good show of it Mom would never buy me anything again.

Really, I had no choice but to whip on some shorts and a T-shirt, throw my hair into a ponytail, and hurry downstairs without even brushing my teeth! As I was heading downstairs, I thought it would serve Julie right if I blasted her with a very breathy "hellllooo."

I didn't get a chance, though, because Julie shot down the driveway as soon as she saw me. I practically had to break my neck to stay even ten paces behind her, which was as close as she wanted me to get, evidently, since she never slowed down OR looked back.

We jogged down to the end of Mill Street, a pretty long street, and then turned the corner onto Hobby Lane. Julie went the length of Hobby Lane, then turned back and did the street again. I just followed along slowly—trying to catch my breath so I could run *with* my sister instead of *after* her. But when we got to the corner of Hobby and Johnstone, she doubled *back* to run down Hobby Lane *again*.

"What gives?" I called as she passed me. She didn't answer. But she really didn't have to because just about then, Lyle Bernard came out of his garage on a bike.

I have to admit that seeing something that looks like Lyle makes getting out of bed ridiculously early in the morning almost worth it. That's because there's only one word to describe him: *sleek*.

His tan legs show off long, defined muscles, but not the bulging bodybuilder type.

His shoulder-length hair is thick, straight, and the color of coffee—without cream. His face is sculpted looking. There isn't a line in is body that looks out of place. And seeing Lyle today made me realize what a long way those twelve-year-old guys, like his brother Phillip, have to go. Maybe I'm gathering data on the wrong-aged subjects. . . .

Lyle paused at the end of the driveway to pull his hair back into a short ponytail before putting on his helmet. Julie picked up her pace about then and in a second she was jogging in place in front of him as he fastened his chinstrap.

I was too far away to hear what they were saying, so I shifted into high gear. I swear I've never run so fast in my entire life! My legs felt like they were being sunburned from the inside out. The sting of a new-shoe blister on my right heel made every step excruciating. Sweat poured down my forehead at white-water speed and blurred my vision. But did I let ~~a little~~ major discomfort get in the way of potential eavesdropping? No!

Finally, I got close enough to hear what they were saying.

"Really?" asked Julie.

"Yep," said Lyle. Then he hopped onto his bike. He looked back over his shoulder and waved as he rolled away.

Julie turned around and slowly jogged backward, watching him.

"So—you—like—Lyle?" I panted. It was what Mrs. Hill calls "a rhetorical question."

"Shut up, Kara," said Julie. She left me in her dust. Again.

But at least I had a chance to do some unobtrusive observing of Lyle. With Julie talking to him, he didn't even notice me staring. When I thought about how easy it was for me to stare unnoticed, it was kind of depressing. . . .

Anyway, there's no point in doing any future "observations" on Lyle, unless it's for my own personal enjoyment, because Julie is obviously in love with him. But here's the data I got on him. Just in case.

Subject #13: LYLE BERNARD
Data Collected on: 1/22   Status: Available, but not to me
Hair: Brown. Long
Eyes: Dark brown. Well-lashed
Eyebrows: Nice. Almost perfect, like his brother, Phillip's
Body Type: Lean but muscular
Age: 16
Nice-o-meter: ☺☺☺☺
Interest Level: ♥♥♥♥♥ (If Julie decides she's not into him)
Fast Fact: Athletic

At school. Before the first bell.

I got to school early today and I'm soooo glad I did because I would have missed all of the action if I hadn't.

But I didn't miss Alex Brantley getting out of his dad's

SUV. And I didn't miss seeing him walk up to Maybelline like he does every morning and I didn't miss seeing him say something to her that made her start crying, grab The Sponge, and hurry away. And I didn't miss seeing Alex Brantley turn to Alex Langford, shrug, and start motioning with his hands like he was explaining something. But you really don't have to explain anything when you've said something to the girl you've been going with for almost three years that makes her cry, grab her BFF, and run away. Because everyone knows what that means. Alex Brantley just broke up with Maybelline.

First period

Maybelline still hasn't come to class. I bet she's in the bathroom doing one of two things:

1. Bawling her eyes out (What girl wouldn't when she loses the cutest boy in school?)
2. Reapplying the makeup that was ruined when she was bawling her eyes out

I'm sure it must be upsetting for Maybelline to lose a catch like Alex, but since she's kind of a rotten person, it's hard to feel bad for her.

And I'm thinking this breakup is a good thing for every other girl at Spring Valley Middle. Alex Brantley, the best looking boy in school, is now available.

Third period

Just turned in my work. It was hard to get it done, let me tell you, with all the sniffing that was going on behind me. But at least Maybelline has her head on her desk with her eyes closed, so it's safe to write.

Since Alex is a free man, I've been observing him again. He doesn't seem upset at all. He even caught me looking at him once and smiled. It wasn't a really great smile though. His eyes didn't light up. They still looked like they were focusing on a dictionary.

Subject #2: ALEX BRANTLEY (Card 2)

Data Collected on: 1/22   Status: Available!

Hair: Black and thick

Eyes: Brown

Eyebrows: Perfect

Body Type: Athletic

Age: 13

Nice-o-meter: ☺☺☺☺

Interest Level: ♥♥♥♥

Fast Fact: Interest in AB just went up now that he has dumped his worst quality: Maybelline! She was weighing him down.

Lunch

Well, that didn't take long. I guess The Sponge so desperately wants to be like Maybelline that she just broke up with Alex Langford! I was walking behind her and Maybelline and I heard her say, "Isn't this great, Colleen? Now that we're both single, we can do a lot more stuff together."

I guess this breakup is good news for all vapid (new vocab word) girls searching for soul mates who have no personality whatsoever — like Alex Langford.

I'd think anyone would be happy to be free of The Sponge, but Alex actually looks bummed about it. And I have to say that The Sponge is being pretty harsh. She walked by him in the cafeteria talking loudly about there being "more fish in the sea." I swear there was a tear in Alex's eye when he jerked his head to the side, trying to pretend he didn't see her.

I found myself feeling a little sorry for him. I guess vapid people have feelings, too.

Subject #6: ALEX LANGFORD (Card 2)
Data Collected on: 1/22   Status: Available
Hair: Dark brown
Eyes: Dark brown
Eyebrows: Ho-Hum
Body Type: Ho-Hum
Age: 12
Nice-o-meter: ☺☺☺
Interest level: Still 0

Bedtime

Things are looking up! I just had my first really normal conversation with Tabbi since she started dating Evan. I realized that even though it's uncomfortable for me to be around my crush, I still need Tabbi as my best friend. I came to this realization after hearing the juiciest gossip of the year. I had to tell someone. And it had to be Tabs.

See, Julie just asked me, "Do you know a guy named Alex Brantley?"

I said, "Yeah, why?"

"Amanda Bodie can't stop talking about him."

"The cheerleader? Isn't she in ninth grade?"

"Yeah and yeah. Everyone's teasing her because she's dating a middle schooler. But Amanda says she doesn't care. She says Alex is hotter than anyone at the high school. So . . ."

"So what?"

"So tell me," said Julie. "Is it true? Is the guy really that hot?"

"Hotter than Mouth of Hades chili at Texas Steakranch," I said.

"Bring tears to your eyes?"

"Oh yeah."

Then Julie made me dig out last year's yearbook and show her a picture. When she saw it she said, "Yummy."

"Julie!" I said. "You're drooling over a sixth grader!"

Julie tossed her ponytail. I hate when she does that. "Am not. He's in seventh grade now."

And I realized I really didn't want to talk to Julie anymore because I had to call Tabbi and give her the dirt. Alex broke up with Maybelline for an older woman!

Tabs was thrilled to be one of the first to know. We talked just like old times. We agreed that it wouldn't be so weird if they were old like my aunt Mona and uncle Mike (he's thirty-eight and she's forty). I mean after they reach a certain point, all adults kind of seem the same age. But Alex is only thirteen and his new girlfriend is fifteen! She can drive! We only quit talking when Tabs's mom yanked the phone out of her hand. Like I said, she's waaay strict about bedtime.

So now I'm sitting here wondering about how Alex's choice of an older woman impacts my soul mate search. While I'm secretly glad that Maybelline is getting her due (okay, not so secretly), I also find this totally unfair! Alex is the cutest boy in seventh grade and possibly the cutest boy in the ENTIRE school and I can't even compete with other seventh graders for guys like him, so how am I going to compete with ninth graders? Especially one who looks great in a skimpy cheerleading uniform. ☹ Rah! Rah! Blah!

Seriously, what if Amanda is Alex's one and only soul mate? I mean, if my one and only soul mate is two years younger than *me*, then *he's* still running around with those little fifth graders on the elementary school playground. And I can tell you one thing. There's no way I'm going out with a fifth grader. Seriously. I'm taller than most of the guys in my own grade as it is. So if my soul mate is down there in fifth grade right now, I guess I'm just going to have to miss out on him.

Tuesday, January 23
After breakfast

Day two of self-induced torture. Just got back from my run with Julie. We took the same route. Right by Lyle's house. It's pretty obvious that I'm not cut out for running. I'm sore all over! I mentioned this at breakfast and Mom said, "You haven't had those seventy-eight-dollar shoes long enough to know. Have you, Kara?"

When she said "have," she stretched out the aaaaaaaaaaaa sound in a way that means the same thing to every daughter on the planet: *The answer better be NO!*

First period

I wonder if Maybelline knows yet that she was dumped for an older woman? She's still sniffing, but no more or less than yesterday.

Second period

That sniffing is getting on my nerves. I've been trying to ignore it, but it's difficult to *sniff* write *sniff* when *sniff* every *sniff* other *sniff* second *sniff* you *sniff* hear *sniff* a *sniff.*

Fourth period

It's hard to pay attention to Mr. DeLacey anymore. I can't even stand to look at him after the whole survey incident. But know what makes it even harder? *Sniffing.* Right behind your head. I know I'm not the only one who hates sniffing either because I did an experiment. I sniffed about three times in Mrs. Hill's class, and Cory Livingston turned around and said, "Get a tissue already, Kara!"

Sixth period

Maybe it was the sniffing. Maybe it was the fact that Maybelline was so mean that time she called me just to say, "What's wrong, Kara? All those A's can't help you figure out how to get a boyfriend?" Maybe I have completely lost my mind. All I know is I shouldn't have said what I just said.

The only thing I'm thankful for right now is that Maybelline thinks she's too cool to be in the band. The band room is my new sanctuary. Tomorrow I'm going to guidance to see if I can have all of my classes changed to band. If I claim to want a career in music, they can't make me take English and algebra, can they?

STUDENT NAME		HOMEROOM		GRADE
MCALLISTER, KARA		BR		7
COURSE	PERIOD	DAYS	ROOM #	TEACHER
BAND	1	MTWRF	BR	WALDORF
BAND	2	MTWRF	BR	WALDORF
BAND	3	MTWRF	BR	WALDORF
LUNCH	4	MTWRF	CAF	
BAND	5	MTWRF	BR	WALDORF
BAND	6	MTWRF	BR	WALDORF
BAND	7	MTWRF	BR	WALDORF

The minute I got home from school

Tabbi called just as I stepped off of the bus. That girl has perfect timing.

Tabs: Maybelline is going to kill you.

Me: I know.

Tabs: No one can believe you said that to her.

Me: Including me.

Tabs: What are you going to do?

Me: I don't know. Maybe when she thinks about it, she'll know I only said it to her because of what she said to me. I mean, if she can get away with it, why can't I?

Tabs: She's Maybelline. You're not.

Me: I know.

Tabs: Oh, Kara. I think you're going to be in for a long day tomorrow. But Evan and I will stick by you.

Me: I know. Thanks, Tabs.

Tabs: Welcome. See you tomorrow. Unless Maybelline sees you first. Then you're dead.

Me: I know. . . . Bye.

Bedtime. According to me. Because being awake isn't doing anything for me. Unless scientists have suddenly discovered that worry is good for the body.

Life is really not fair. I mean it *finally* looks like karma has caught up with Maybelline for being such a rotten person, and then I have to go and wave a big red cape in its direction. I may as well have yelled, "Hey, Karma! Lower your head and charge this way!"

Why couldn't I have just quietly enjoyed the experience

of Maybelline getting dumped from the safety of my desk? Oh. That's right. Because it wasn't very quiet at my desk because of all of that SNIFFING! The sniffing drove me to it. I swear.

But did I have to turn around and say, "What's wrong, Colleen? All that makeup not helping you get a boyfriend?"

Every now and then, my dad will say something about "jealousy rearing its ugly head." I wonder if Dad knows that revenge has an ugly head, too. I saw revenge rear its ugly head when Maybelline jerked her head from her desk after I stupidly opened my mouth about her boyfriend status.

Did you know revenge has cold, evil-looking eyes under green eye shadow? It also has a perfectly formed mouth with beautiful teeth. And it can make the most innocent-sounding sentences make your blood run cold when it says, "Oh, I'll get another boyfriend, Kara. Don't you worry."

Know what? I'm worried.

Wednesday, January 24
Before breakfast

Complained of hurt knee and begged out of running but promised to go tomorrow. Didn't sleep well last night.

Sixth period

Today Tabbi met Evan in front of school and wrote *Property of Tabbi Reddy* on his hand, like she's done every day since they started going out. She added a big heart with a red Sharpie in honor of their two-week anniversary. That's supposedly some kind of milestone. As she gushed about how it has been the best two weeks of her life, it made me a little sick. Just like it does every time she gushes about Evan. So, you see, today started out like a very normal day.

Surprisingly, even Maybelline was acting fairly normal. Sure she glared at me when I got out of Dad's Honda, but she pretty much does that every day. And she "accidentally" kicked my desk a few times when she got up to sashay to the pencil sharpener, but she does that about every day, too. And at least she'd stopped that annoying sniffing! I wondered if things between Maybelline and me weren't going to be *too* too much worse than they already were. I even thought maybe my confronting her yesterday was a *good* thing. Hey—I'd rather have my desk kicked a few dozen times than listen to sniffing all day long.

But that was before lunch.

At lunch I sat with Anna Johnstone and Dianna Leroy, just like old times. I *really* did not want to sit with Tabs and Evan on their highly publicized "two-week anniversary." I noticed Anna was reading a book called *The Mediator*, which is about a girl who has a crush on a handsome ghost who is, like, two hundred years old. I loved that book! So we got into this great (but weird) conversation about the top ten ghosts you would consider going out with, and lunch flew by without my taking notes on any more subjects. So it wasn't until fourth period that I got clued in that something was very wrong with my world. Here were my clues:

1. Tabbi did not come to class.
2. Evan did. But when he raised his hand to answer a question, it did not have writing on it. All that was left of his temporary tattoo was a pale pink blob where the heart used to be.
3. After class, Evan started walking toward my desk. "Where's Tabs?" I asked. He shrugged! Then he passed my desk and stopped at Maybelline's.
4. Next, Evan picked up Maybelline's books and walked toward the door!!!
5. And Maybelline hooked her hand in the crook of Evan's arm and walked with him!!!!

Maybelline looked over her shoulder and gave me a big, exaggerated wink. "Told you I'd get a boyfriend," she said.

I couldn't move. All of the times that I'd felt sick listening to Tabbi talk about Evan didn't compare to how seriously ill

I felt at that very moment. It was like someone had spread Gorilla Glue on my butt and I was going to be stuck in my desk forever. I was cold. And shaky. Tabbi was somewhere (probably home) crying her eyes out, and it was all thanks to me. Maybelline wanted to get back at me, and since I didn't have a boyfriend she stole my best friend's.

I might have stayed in that seat forever if fifth period hadn't started filing in and Mia Willers hadn't said, "Get out of my seat, girl, before I dump you out."

Now I'm in the instrument room pretending to fix a stuck valve. Even though I could get suspended for it, I'm taking out my cell phone and dialing Tabbi's number.

She doesn't answer.

I wonder how long I can stay back here before Mr. Waldorf notices? I do not feel like making a joyful noise today. . . .

Bedtime

After trying Tabbi's cell a thousand times and only getting voicemail, I was finally able to reach her by calling her home number and talking to her mom first.

As soon as I said hello, Tabs started sobbing. It was hard to understand what she was saying, exactly, but eventually I managed to get the whole story.

Basically, Evan is a jerk and Maybelline is a fiend. Get

this—at lunch, Maybelline just sashayed up to Evan and Tabs while they were *celebrating their two-week anniversary* and asked Evan to go to the spring dance with her! And right in front of Tabbi, Evan said yes.

Tabs said she asked Evan if he liked Maybelline so much, why hadn't he just asked her out a long time ago? He said he would have, but he didn't think a girl as pretty as Maybelline would say yes!!!

Poor Tabbi. She was all tears. "You're still looking for your soul mate, Kara, but I'd already *found* mine. Maybelline didn't steal my boyfriend, she stole part of my *soul*."

I feel like the worst friend in the world. If I hadn't been having that ridiculous conversation about dead hotties, I'd have noticed my best friend running from the cafeteria in tears.

I'll tell you what, though. Even when Maybelline does dump Evan—and I'm sure she will since he's obviously (to everyone but him) her rebound guy—I am done researching him. There are some things you never know . . . but I know for sure that my one and only true soul mate will not be someone who treats people like Evan treated Tabbi. I honestly can't believe that I used to like that guy!

I guess if Evan and Tabs weren't meant to be, it's good for Evan that he figured it out before he got his hand tattooed.

Thursday, January 25
Lunch

James and The Vine are no longer going out. This status change doesn't have nearly as much YAY power as Alex's did, but in the interest of being objective with this study, I need to note it anyway. I don't know how he managed to disentangle himself, but Gina is now ignoring James and openly creeping around other guys.

And though it's still hard to imagine how I could ever like someone who willingly let himself fall into The Vine's clutches, it is easier to observe James now that he's free.

One thing I just noticed about him, for example, is that he no longer has a unibrow. I heard him telling Alex L that his mom plucked it for him. My first thought was: Eww! I couldn't really believe that he admitted this. Then again, it was so obvious that it had been plucked—since now he has *two* eyebrows instead of *one*—that I guess he may as well have.

Before

After

And speaking of admitting things, I have to admit that James looks a lot cuter these days. It might be that he walks differently. Like he's more confident or something. His new duo-browed look doesn't hurt, either.

I pointed this out to Tabs, who agreed that he was cuter, but argued that he still wasn't nearly as cute as Evan, before she ran to the restroom teary-eyed.

Subject #3: JAMES POWALSKI (Card 3)
Data Collected on: 1/25   Status: Available
Hair: Wavy and black
Eyes: Brown
Eyebrows: Now there are two!
Body type: Tall and scrawny
Age: 13
Nice-o-meter: ☺☺
Interest Level: 0
Observations: James looks better than he used to.
Fast Fact: His armpits have finally met their savior: deodorant!

After school

Maybelline is making sure to flaunt her new status as Evan's girlfriend every chance she gets. So today has been particularly rough for Tabbi. It's really, really hard to see your BFF looking so sad.

Friday, January 26
Before first bell

Passed Dylan Hudson in the hall this morning and thought I may as well unobtrusively observe him then and there since I have NO classes with him and rarely get a chance to even see him because he is SO popular and SO athletic that he's always barricaded by fans. He's one of those guys I never really think about. After all, he hasn't said so much as "hi" to me since he moved here in fifth grade. He thinks he's too cool to speak to girls like me (he is). But there are plenty of girls he does talk to and he's always dating one of them. If it's not the most popular girl in seventh grade, it's the most popular girl in eighth or even sixth. Age doesn't matter to Dylan. Popularity does.

I whirled around and started casually following him while trying to go unnoticed. As we walked toward the gym (he must have PE first period) about a million people spoke to Dylan.

"'Sup, Dylan?"

"Yo."

"Great game, Dylan."

"You're d'man."

"Dude."

But no one spoke to me. It turns out that when you're walking in the wake of someone as magnificently popular as Dylan, you don't have to worry about getting noticed. When I thought about how easy it was to go unnoticed in Dylan's wake, it was kind of depressing. . . .

Dylan eventually went through the doors of the gym, so I stopped following him. I've done a lot of things I normally wouldn't do for this research project already, but I draw the line at spending extra time with Coach Little.

Subject #14: DYLAN HUDSON

Data Collected on: 1/26   Status: Never available for
                                 more than ½ a day
Hair: Thick, gorgeous, blondish

Eyes: Dark brown

Eyebrows: Perfect like the rest of him

Body Type: See "Eyebrows"

Age: 13

Nice-o-meter: ☺

Interest Level: ♥

Third period

Guess how I found out James Powalski is no longer single? By reading his hand! That's right, James strolled into second period this morning with *Property of Tabbi Reddy* written on his hand. I whirled around to look at Tabbi, but she wasn't looking at me. She was staring at James and silently giggling. Blech! You'd think it'd take longer than forty-eight hours to get over being dumped by your soul mate.

I managed to ask Tabs about it when we were changing classes. She impatiently ran fingers through her short blond hair and said, "I was wrong about Evan. Anyway, just yesterday you mentioned that James has gotten a lot cuter."

I admitted that I had. But I added that I couldn't see how she could like someone who used to let The Vine climb all over him. She rolled her eyes and said, "You can't judge people by who they *used* to date, Kara. I certainly don't want to be judged by *that* loser."

She nodded toward Evan as we entered Mrs. Hill's class. He had his arms locked with Maybelline's. Then Tabs stalked away to wrap her arm around James's shoulders. I guess they had gotten cold after The Vine uprooted.

Even though I was annoyed with her, I didn't have the heart to tell Tabbi that standing arm in arm with a girl like Maybelline hardly makes Evan look like a loser.

Lunch

My social life has hit rock bottom. I, Kara McAllister, am sitting alone at a table. This wouldn't be so bad if the table didn't have room for twelve. And if it wasn't located in the cafeteria surrounded by full tables, one of which Tabbi is sitting at with James and his friends.

I'm starting to wonder if I'm going about this research all wrong. Maybe instead of observing boys, I should be observing girls. Girls who've had relationship success, that is. Maybe by watching them, I can figure out what I need to do to get a boyfriend! I may as well start now. When you're alone at a table for twelve, it's crucial that you look busy. Like you've actually *chosen* exile.

Gina Johns (AKA: The Vine) is newly single and she's probably already planning to do whatever it is she does to get boys to like her. So I'm starting with her. She's currently giving Alex L a hug. Man, does he look uncomfortable. His eyes keep wandering over to Tiffany Davidson (AKA: The Sponge) who either

(a) is ignoring him.

or

(b) has forgotten he exists.

Wait. Alex is tapping Gina on the shoulder. She's letting go. Now he's backing away from her. He must have told her he had to go or something, to get her to loosen her grip. The Vine doesn't seem bothered by this obvious (and public) rejection! She's heading toward some guy whose name I can't remember. He seems to like being hugged like a stuffed toy.

Girl Subject #1: GINA JOHNS
Alias: The Vine
Data Collected on: 1/26   Status: Available
Age: 12
Looks: OK
Popular: N
Unobtrusive observations: Subject was observed hugging various subjects. It was like she was test-driving teddy bears.
Rejection does not bother subject.
Boy attraction method: Hugging

Hmmm. In the time it took me to write this card, The Vine has moved on to yet another boy! There is kind of no point observing her anymore. She just does the same thing over and over again. So I'm moving on to Maybelline. Thanks to Tabbi, I already know what her boy attraction method is. Plus, I have a great view of her.

You know what really stinks? Maybelline doesn't really have to do anything to get attention from boys. Right now she's at the popular table with Evan, who looks completely out of place. The Sponge and three other guys are sitting there, too. Maybelline's talking. And every male at the table is looking at her like her conversation is fascinating. Which has to be a total act. In all of the years I've know her, I've never heard her say a single interesting thing! It's not fair!

Poor Gina has to put all kinds of energy into getting guys to look at her (by getting so close to them that they can't look anywhere else) while Maybelline just sits there. Then when she sees something she wants (Evan) she just walks up and takes it with no effort at all.

Girl Subject #2: COLLEEN McCARVER
AKA: Maybelline
Data Collected on: 1/26   Status: Taken
Age: 12
Looks: Fabulous (Man, do I hate to admit this.)
Popular: Wildly (And this!)
Unobtrusive observations: Subject was observed leaning on the former BF of my BFF.
Even guys who aren't dating Maybelline look at her.
Boy attraction method: Stealing

Whew! Lunch is almost over. If I go to the bathroom before walking s-l-o-w-l-y to class, I can escape my exile now.

Saturday, January 27
After breakfast

Unfortunately for me, Julie even runs on the weekends and guess who is expected to go with her?

It didn't exactly make me feel any better about getting up at the crack of dawn when I realized that Julie looked even *less* happy than usual to see me and my seventy-eight-dollar shoes come down the stairs. As soon as we got out of the driveway, she explained.

"Look, Kara, I know you want to use your new shoes and all, but I need you to stop running with me every morning."

"Why?"

"Because I want to start running with Lyle," she sighed. (I knew it!)

"I can see why—he's totally cute!" I said.

Julie smiled. "I didn't think you noticed stuff like that."

"Of course I do!" I said. "The only reason I even bought these sneakers was to get another chance to see this guy who works at the mall."

Julie laughed and stopped running . . . to hug me!!! Julie's not exactly the touchy-feely type, so I was kind of surprised by the hug.

Then she gave me all of the details about her and Lyle. Last night they went to the movies with a bunch of friends. Julie claims it counts as their first date since Lyle held her hand the whole time.

I was more than happy to agree to give up running! So we devised a plan. I will wear my running shoes to school every day and try to wear them out in a hurry (I know I'll look like a dork, but it will be worth it if I can stop waking up at 6:00 a.m.). Meanwhile, she'll try to think of some way for me to get out of our morning run without getting either of us into trouble.

We ended up at Lyle's house, of course, and he came down the driveway in brand-new running shoes! He gave Julie a quick kiss before they took off, leaving me behind— a third wheel rolling along in the distance. I didn't mind, though. Maybe Lyle is Julie's soul mate and maybe I'll find one too when I'm sixteen. And I was also happy to know that one of my plans actually seemed to work, even if it didn't work for *me*, because it looks like buying new running shoes might be helping *Lyle* find a soul mate!

Afternoon

Since Julie is the only person anywhere near my age that I've seen today, I thought I might as well make a card on her. The method she uses to attract boys is now pretty obvious to me.

The more I think about it, the more I'm not sure this particular research strategy is worth continuing. So far, I've observed three girls. One gets boys to notice her by hugging them. One gets boys to notice her by being beautiful. One gets boys to notice her by running.

I know for sure that none of these boy-getting strategies will work for me. First of all, I can't help my looks. There's nothing I can do to make myself look like Maybelline. Second, I can't stand running. I'm RELIEVED that Julie doesn't want to run with me anymore! Finally, I am not about to go hugging random boys to get one to notice me. That's just not me. If I started acting like that, I wouldn't be Kara.

Sunday, January 28
Bedtime

Tabbi called me last night to see if I wanted to go to a get-together at Dianna Leroy's and to ask if she could spend the night afterward. We always try to have sleepovers at my house because it's not much fun at Tabs's, thanks to her mom's obsession with early bedtimes. I said yes, of course.

Anyway, I'd just gotten my fourth e-mail from Bebe Truelove, along with another ad.

To: Kara M <Craftychick@mailquickly.com>
From: BebeTruelove <bebe@bebetruelove.com>
Subject: Tip #4

Dear Soul Mate Seeker,

It's not *what* you look like, it's *how* you look. No man can resist the following trick!

Tip #4: Give him the bug eye.

Good Luck in Love,
Bebe

I took Bebe's advice to mean that you go up to a guy and tell him you have a bug in your eye. Then when he touches your face to help you get it out . . . sparks will fly! Maybe.

So I went to Dianna's with Tabs (who spent the entire time with James) just to try the Bug Eye out on a few guys. It didn't work the way I thought it would at all.

RESEARCH RESULTS: The Bug Eye Experiment

If this experiment is any indication of my romantic future, I'm doomed.

Responses to the "Bug Eye Test"
Subject #2: "Bathroom's that way."
Subject #1: "Get Tabbi to help you with that."
Subject #4: "I hate when that happens!"
Subject #6: "Ewww."

Gave up after giving test to four subjects.

After the party I found out why the Bug Eye didn't work for me. As soon as we got to my room, I turned to Tabs and said, "Did you have to spend *every minute* with James?"

"Yep," she laughed. "I knew I'd get to talk to you *after* the party."

I groaned. "I'm tired of being the only one who doesn't have a date. It's so awkward."

"First of all, you weren't the only one without a date. Only two people there had dates. And second, if you want a date, why don't you try harder to get guys to notice you?"

"I am trying!" I practically yelled. "I even did the Bug Eye test during the party and no one was interested."

"Kara . . . What'd you do?"

"I went up to four different guys and told them a bug had just flown into my eye. And none of them touched my face like they were supposed to or got any closer to me to help me out."

Tabbi tugged at her bottom eyelid until I could see the slimy, red-veined part. My response was pretty much the same as Subject #6's.

"You didn't do *this*, did you?" she asked.

I nodded weakly.

Tabs rolled back on the bed and laughed. And laughed. And laughed. For me, it was not the feel-good moment of the year. When she caught her breath she sat up. "What guy wants to look at *that*? I don't know what you read, but when it comes to guys, this is what *the bug eye* means."

Then Tabs tilted her head down, while glancing up and batting her eyelashes. She looked pretty cute. I'm fairly certain I've never had that look on my face in my life.

Maybe I'll practice in front of the mirror. But even if I do, somehow I think it's gonna take a lot more courage for me to look at a guy the way Tabbi just showed me than to walk up and ask for his assistance in removing an insect from my cornea.

```
              WEEK 4: RESEARCH REVIEW
           # of boy subjects observed: 6
           # of girl subjects observed: 3

   Findings: Nothing. No closer to discovering soul
         mate. Decided to interact with subjects
                  by performing test.

     Bebe Truelove's Tip #4: Give him the bug eye.
         (Humiliate yourself, in other words.)

              Data Collection Methods:
           observation, social experiment
```

Monday, January 29
The boys' room. Really.

Before today, I guess my lowest point was finding out that Evan liked Tabbi. But at least I got to be miserable about their relationship in the confines of my own (very cool) room. Now I am forced to be miserable in the worst possible of all public places: a restroom.

One that isn't exactly public unless you have something I don't have: a Y chromosome.

I cannot believe my research has caused me to sink to such levels! I mean, if I hadn't been using the last few minutes of third period before the lunch bell to continue my unobtrusive observations, I would have been able to go to my grave saying I had never seen a urinal. Not now.

Unfortunately, in third period, I was so busy concentrating on my research that I didn't notice Maybelline get up from her desk. After all, she's been sashaying back and forth to the pencil sharpener, smacking gum and trying to get certain people (Alex) to notice her again, even though she's supposedly been in love with someone else (Evan) for days. So it took me a second to realize what was happening when I heard a *smack* right above my desk, and my research notebook was suddenly in Maybelline's red-nailed clutches! Why'd I have to write *Soul Observations* on the cover? I guess it's better than what I was going to write (*Soul Mate Observations*). Fortunately, I realized that only one of the guys could possibly be my soul mate, but they are all souls.

"What's this, *Scar-a*?" she asked. (I can't believe she has a nickname for me. The nerve!) I was too panicked to give a good smart-aleck response. Can you imagine how miserable my life would be if it got out that I'd been taking notes on the boys at my school? Even worse, I think it's safe to say that if loyal, wonderful Tabbi saw what I wrote about Evan — our friendship would be over. I never want that to happen.

Luckily for me, however, my mom has what she calls a

"no talon" policy. She pretty much insists that our fingernails "don't get too long to be practical." So when it came down to the tug-of-war over *Soul Observations*, I had the advantage. My opponent let go when she broke a nail.

At that point, I heard the first ping of the lunch bell. I knew this meant Maybelline was about to have a whole forty-five minutes to torment me. I clutched the book to my chest (what there is of it) and ran out the door, leaving my purse and backpack behind, which is fine. I'll pick them up when I go back to Mrs. Hill to give her an excuse about why I bolted. Hopefully, if I tell her I had diarrhea or something, she won't want many details. Most people don't when it comes to diarrhea.

I hurried down the hall looking for some place Maybelline wouldn't find me. None of the classrooms were really safe since they all have those big windows in the doors. Then I saw the perfect door. A door without a window. A door that opened into the one place someone as prissy as Maybelline wouldn't go: the boys' room!

Which is where I am right now.

Is it too much to hope that the guys at Spring Valley Middle all have abnormally large bladders due to some freakish thing in our community, like particularly loud police sirens or something? Maybe they can hold it for a whole lunch period. I will die if anyone sees me in here!!!!!

I don't expect to enjoy spending most of an hour sitting

on a toilet. (With my pants *on*—I'm using it like a chair.) Actually, the stall is kind of like a mini office—except the memos on the walls here are less . . . well . . . professional. Now that I think about it, I'm pretty sure that whoever invented the office cubicle was sitting on the toilet when the inspiration hit. So since I'm stuck in here anyway, I may as well continue my research. If someone does happen to come in, who knows what I'll overhear.

Oof! Someone's coming!

The boys' room. Still.

If you ever want to be disillusioned by someone you once thought was cool and maybe even good-looking in an off-beat way, just spend some time alone with him in a bathroom. Because that's how I realized that Malcolm Maxwell is definitely not—and never will be—my soul mate.

Here's what happened: Malcolm came into the stall next to me and sat down. (I knew he was sitting because his feet were pointing toward the door and I knew it was Malcolm because I recognized the graffiti on his high-tops.)

Of course, realizing that people could be recognized by their shoes alone made me panic for a sec. Then I remembered that, in an effort to wear them out faster, I'd worn my gender-neutral white and gray running shoes. (Thank goodness the store was out of the ones with the shimmery purple swoosh.)

But just when I thought my identity was safe, Malcolm said, "Dude, there's no roll in here. Pass the paper."

I panicked. The blood drumming in my ears was as loud as Malcolm rapping on his snare during band. I imagined him seeing the Frosted Pink Posy polish on my practical, stubby nails as I handed over the paper he needed. Would he then demand to know which girl was on the other side of the stall wall? What would everyone do when they found out I was hiding in the boys' room?

Thankfully, the next thing he said was, "Never mind, dude. I found a gum wrapper." Then he chuckled.

You can see why I have issues with Malcolm now. I could tell that he needed a lot more coverage than what could be had from a tiny wrapper. And I did NOT hear the sink running after he left the stall. Eww.

I can't imagine that my one and only true soul mate will be someone who sends a gum wrapper in to do what is clearly a two-ply job. Talk about lack of perspective! So Malcolm is off of the list.

And even though the data I collected is somewhat disturbing, I have to say that the boys' room *is* a great place to conduct research, because Malcolm said seventeen words to me when he thought I was a guy in the next stall and before that, he'd only said one. So now I have seventeen times as much information as I normally would, just because he didn't know he was talking to a girl.

Okay. The bell is going to ring in a few minutes. Now that I'm alone, I'd better go peek around the door. If no one is in the hall—I'm outta here!

Tuesday, January 30
After school

School today would have been a real nightmare if it hadn't been for Evan. I hadn't even been at school for five minutes before Maybelline started with me. I swear she was waiting for me in the courtyard like a predator stalking its home territory. Evan was right at her side.

I knew she hadn't had time to read any of my data yesterday, but unfortunately she'd gotten a good look at the title of my research journal.

"So, Kara, did you bring that book you're writing with you today?" (I had the sense to leave it home.) I shook my head. "I'd like to read it," she continued, looking smug.

I told her it was private.

She stepped closer to me, pulling Evan behind her by his shirt. "I saw that you're calling it *Soul Observations*." She rolled her eyes, smacked her chewing gum, and raised her voice so that everyone standing there could hear her.

"Who do you think you are, Kara? God?"

I shook my head but couldn't say anything.

I hate myself for it, but I get really intimidated by girls like Maybelline. She's pretty and popular. And even though I like who I am just fine, I feel that other people like her better, and that makes me not want to get into arguments with her in front of the whole student body. So I just stood there frozen, my heart beating rabbit fast.

"Kara thinks she's God! Kara thinks she's better than us. Read it in her book!"

I could feel everyone's eyes on me and I knew that they'd all heard her because it was that awkward kind of I-don't-wanna-miss-a-word-of-this-smackdown silence. Then I heard a very beautiful sound and it came from Evan, of all people.

"Cut it out, Colleen," he said quietly.

"Since when do you tell me what to do, loser?" asked Maybelline.

Evan looked down. "You don't have to be cruel."

Suddenly Maybelline turned all of her meanness onto poor Evan. It was safe for me to walk away at that point. So I did. But I could hear Maybelline squawking at him like a mad chicken, though I couldn't make out the words enough to tell if she was breaking up with him or not. I'm guessing Evan is safe until she finds a replacement. Maybelline isn't going to be caught dead without a boyfriend.

I hope Maybelline breaks up with Evan! Is that wrong? And is it wrong to hope that I'll find out he really did have a good reason for breaking up with Tabs? And to hope that she'll decide that she's so happy with her new boyfriend that she doesn't mind letting me have her old one? I mean, it's hard to keep thinking of Evan as a jerk when he was willing to stand up for me. Would a jerk do that? I think not!

Subject #1: EVAN CARLSON (Card 3)
Data Collected on: 1/30   Status: Stolen!
Hair: Sideburns! Looks better now that he's with M
Eyes: Look even better now that he's with M
Eyebrows: Look even better now that he's with M
Body Type: Looks pretty hot standing next to M
Age: 12
Nice-o-meter: ☺☺☺☺
Interest Level: ?
Fatal Flaw: Maybelline

Wednesday, January 31
Homework time

Note: It's hard to follow through with making "unobtrusive observations" when you yourself are being not-so-unobtrusively observed. Maybelline is just dying to get her hands on my research journal. I can literally feel her breath on my neck every time I reach into my backpack. So I figured I might as well put my soul mate research aside for a while and concentrate on the science fair project, which is due in only six days.

The problem is this: My surveys are worthless and I haven't thought of a new project yet. So I'm heading to the "family computer located in a high-traffic area" to poke around on the Internet and try to find a cool experiment that I can do in, like, a day.

Homework time. Still.

The Good News: I found a great project—the perfect combination of *looking* complicated but actually only involving a few easy steps! All I need is a few packs of Alka-Seltzer tablets. Perfect!

The Bad News: When I asked Mom, who wasn't doing *anything* but reading her book-club book, if she would take me to the store to get supplies, she looked up and asked, "When's the project due?" I told her. She looked back down at her book. "And when was the project assigned?"

She didn't even look up again when I answered that question. "You're just going to have to use what you can find around the house. I'm not making a special trip to the store for someone who doesn't plan."

I tried to appeal to Mom's sympathy by reminding her of the whole Evil-DeLacey-Survey-Stealer saga, but when she asked, "So when did you get the surveys back and realize you couldn't use them?" I knew I was sunk. It was thirteen days ago. At that point Mom's only comment was to silently turn the page.

Unfortunately for me, my parents don't really have any cool science-experiment type stuff around the house. Here's what we do have: books, craft supplies, and a recycling bin full of Diet Coke cans. But I went rummaging through the pantry anyway, pulling out anything I thought I could possibly transform into a science experiment. In the end, it amounted to a box of baking soda (too lame to build a volcano though), some packets of Kool-Aid, and a bag of curly pasta. Einstein couldn't come up with an experiment that uses those things.

It was hopeless. I flopped down on the sofa and stared at the ceiling. I flipped over and stared at the rug. I think staring at floors and ceilings is a sign of clinical depression or something. If it isn't, it should be. Because realizing that you are kissing your science grade good-bye (along with any hope of unlimited texting) is pretty darn depressing.

I tried to think about science experiments I'd done in the past. Ones that worked. And suddenly I remembered something we always had a ton of in the backyard: earthworms! I'd used them for my fourth-grade science fair project to show how plants that are potted with earthworms grow better than those potted without.

I went out and dug around in the backyard. Thirty minutes later I had a box of baking soda, some packets of Kool-Aid, a bag of curly pasta, and twenty-one wriggling worms! I went to get a notebook from Mom's stockpile of bargain back-to-school supplies so I could start jotting down thoughts. Ironically, she had another notebook exactly like the one I'm using for *Soul Observations*. And this gave me a great idea!

Thursday, February 1
Fifth period

Dear Ms. Sabatino,

You are the coolest teacher ever. I mean, you watch YouTube! And show us cool videos of amazing science stuff.

Did you know that the guys talk about you the same way the girls (except for me, now that I know he has a kinda rotten soul) talk about Mr. DeLacey? Plus, you always wear those funky wedges. They just scream "artsy." Hopefully this means you're going to love my science board. 'Cause next week I'll be turning in the most cool, the most artsy, the most creative science board you've ever seen!

Man! Did you have to pick now to close your laptop and start a lecture?

Signed, but never to be delivered by,

Kara McAllister

After school

Just had a chance to unobtrusively observe Subject #12, Richie Lopez, while he was grocery shopping with his family. You know, I said he doesn't talk much because he doesn't— in school. But he was talking like crazy in Publix. I couldn't understand a word of it! (Which is too bad because I have suffered through two boring years of Español but still can't *comprendo*.) He was talking *that* fast. Of course he was smiling. He looked so, well, cute. Hmmm . . .

Saturday, February 3
Afternoon

So far I've spent the whole weekend with earthworms instead of people. This is not going to help me find a soul mate. I can tell.

Sunday, February 4
After lunch

Bebe Truelove does not get it. I just received her latest tip.

To: Kara M <Craftychick@mailquickly.com>
From: BebeTruelove <bebe@bebetruelove.com>
Subject: Tip #5

Dear Soul Mate Seeker,

You've made your list and you know what you are looking for in a soul mate. Well, look at that list again. Maybe you're being too picky. Love will enter your life if you open the door a little wider.

Tip #5: Be open minded.

Good Luck in Love,

Bebe

I *am* open-minded! The only guys I've closed the door to are James, Evan, Jonah Nate, algebra teachers, Alex L, ones who don't use toilet paper, and anyone who has ever dated The Vine! Geez!

Bedtime

I'm skipping the weekly research review for my boy project because I've been too busy with my science fair project. I didn't have time to collect a ton of data on the worms, but I tried to make up for it by designing an awesome display board. Mom's crafting philosophy is that "a little fringe can dress up anything." (Our lampshades are nonliving proof of this.) But I've found this philosophy useful for school as well. Teachers *love* it when you show enthusiasm for a project by throwing a little extra decoration on it.

Here's what my display board looks like. And it's

multisensory interactive! Notice the scratch-and-sniff areas where I sprinkled some Kool-Aid on two squares of glue. Also—and this is the best part—I took apart a musical birthday card I got last year and glued the sound-making mechanism to the science board. Now it plays the "Chicken Dance" when you open it! Perfect for a project about worms, right?

Hypothesis

Earthworms thrive in tastier soil.

Soil: Does Flavor Affect Worm Growth?

Kool-Aid

Kool-Aid

Scratch and sniff

Scratch and sniff

Dirt

Data

Initial worm weight:
Group 1: 2.12 oz
Group 2: 2.19 oz
Group 3: 2.11 oz

Materials

·21 earthworms
·3 buckets of dirt
·2 packs of drink mix
·1 postage scale

Results

Ending worm weight:
Group 1: 2.10 oz
Group 2: 2.19 oz
Group 3: 2.11 oz

Experiment

Worms are placed in soil to see if taste affects growth.

Procedure:
1. Put dirt into three same-sized buckets.
2. Mix cherry drink mix into one bucket.
3. Mix lime drink mix into one bucket.
4. Leave third bucket plain.
5. Divide worms into three groups of 7.
6. Weigh each group and record weight.
7. Put 7 worms into each bucket.
8. Weigh worms again at the end of experiment and record weight.

Conclusion

Flavored soil has little (if any) effect on worm growth.

Monday, February 5
After school

Turned in science project. It was the best one! When I opened it up, James, who sits in the back row, actually raised his hands over his head (thank goodness he finally discovered deodorant) and started snapping his fingers together like chicken beaks. And Alex L spent an inordinately long time sniffing the lime-scented scratch-and-sniff square. (?) (!)

Found out during second period that Maybelline broke up with Evan over the weekend. I'm sure he saw it coming after bravely defending me. But just like I predicted . . . she made sure she'd latched on to somebody else first. An eighth grader. (She was probably aiming for ninth—just to show Alex—but she had to take what she could get, you know.)

Tuesday, February 6
Fifth period

I, Kara McAllister, am going to die. True, this statement could be made of anyone—and it's actually true of everyone—but I see the future clearly and I know the exact cause of my death. I went ahead and made a death certificate to save my poor parents the trouble.

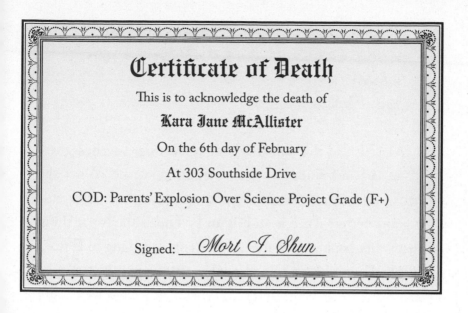

Certificate of Death

This is to acknowledge the death of

Kara Jane McAllister

On the 6th day of February

At 303 Southside Drive

COD: Parents' Explosion Over Science Project Grade (F+)

Signed: _Mort I. Shun_

Unfortunately, it turned out that Ms. Sabatino isn't someone who is easily impressed by Mom's "little bit of fringe" philosophy. Here's what she wrote on the back of my science board.

F+

Kara,
This project is completely different from the one you described on your application! Your artistic display is nice, but your experiment lacks substance. You didn't start it in time to collect any real data. Even worse — adding artificial

flavoring to the soil may actually harm the worms. Did you think of that? See me after school!

Ms. Sabatino

After I read through that tongue-lashing—well, I guess it was a pen-lashing—I sat in stunned silence. What the heck's an F+? Like that little plus sign is going to make failing any better? An F is an F is an F. This is the worst thing that's ever happened to me. My parents are going to F-reak. It'll be F-atal. I have ruined my F-uture!

I was sitting there panicking when I heard a voice calling to me from a distance.

"Kara. Kara?"

Okay, the voice calling my name wasn't so distant from me physically—but I'd let my mind wander far, far away from room 217 while imagining my death.

"Kara McAllister!"

Now the voice sounded irritated. My mind sped back to room 217.

"Kara!" said Ms. Sabatino again. "Release those poor earthworms. They'll probably love it in the courtyard." Ms. Sabatino turned to the class. "Any volunteers to help Kara with these buckets?"

Then a surprising thing happened. A weird, exciting, surprising thing. Two hands shot up. One was attached to

Chip Tyler. The other was attached to Evan! Ms. Sabatino nodded toward Evan, who picked up two of the buckets and headed out of the classroom. I grabbed the third bucket and followed.

Even though it was probably good for Evan to see what it felt like to be dumped, I still felt bad that his girlfriend jilted him for defending me. So as soon as I caught up with him I said, "Sorry about you and Maybelline." (Yeah. I said Maybelline. Oops!)

Evan looked at me for a second and I think the heat coming from my face could have roasted a marshmallow at that point. "I meant to say Colleen," I added quickly.

He looked at the ground and shook his head. "Don't worry about it," he said. Then he chuckled. "Maybelline. I get that. She does wear a lot of the stuff, doesn't she?"

I'm glad he thought it was funny, but I sure didn't. Tabs and I promised that we'd *never* tell other people the nicknames we use. I mean, if it gets back to Maybelline that we call her something other than Colleen, she'll ruin our lives! I begged Evan not to repeat that (instead of denying I said it, like I should have).

He smiled. "Your secret is safe with me." I think he meant it.

I told him again how sorry I was that his relationship was ruined and he said, "It was bound to happen sooner or later. She's not really that nice."

He laughed when I agreed. You know, there aren't many good things I can say about Maybelline, but I have to admit that the few days Evan spent under her discerning eye really helped his appearance. He was wearing cool clothes, had a great haircut, and his sideburns made him look even cuter. Of course, Evan always looked pretty good to me.

I only had one thought on my mind as we walked back to class and that was: *I was right all along! Evan Carlson is supposed to be my soul mate!*

After school. Waiting for Ms. S.

At least having to meet with Ms. S gave me a good excuse to cut my chat with Tabbi short. It was hard to talk to her because the whole time she was blabbing about James I wanted to blurt out, "Since you like James so much, I guess you won't mind if I like Evan."

I never did get the nerve to say it, though. Probably because I already knew what the answer would be.

Bedtime

I really don't feel the need to tell my parents about the dreaded F+ because Ms. Sabatino is going to give me a chance to bring up my grade! The first thing she asked me was, "Why didn't you follow through with the project described on your science fair application?"

"I did follow through," I said. "I distributed one hundred and fifteen surveys, compiled the data, and created a graph."

Ms. Sabatino raised an eyebrow that had been plucked to perfection. "So why didn't you use it for your project?"

"Mr. DeLacey said my sample wasn't large enough."

"Hmmm. He may have had a point. But you could've surveyed more students."

"I know," I sighed.

She crossed her arms and looked at me in a way that means *Keep explaining, kid* to every kid who's ever been in trouble.

"Well, Mr. DeLacey also said there was nothing scientific about the surveys," I continued. "He suggested that I start with something new." I was tempted to tell her that Mr. D had also predicted I'd thank him when I got a grade higher than an F. Shows how much he knows about the future, because I'm not wasting a single breath to thank him for that little plus sign.

Ms. Sabatino stood up and started pacing. "What subject does Mr. DeLacey teach?"

"Algebra."

"I fail to see why you considered his opinion without asking mine."

Once she put it that way, I failed to see it, too. What good was Mr. DeLacey's opinion? So far, the only thing it had gotten me was after-school detention and the lowest grade of my school career.

"If you had come to me, I'd have encouraged you to keep the theme of your original project, even if you had to adjust it a bit. Scientists do their best work on topics that interest them. And I have a feeling you're a lot more interested in relationships than earthworms."

No argument there, but it did make me blush. I can handle a little embarrassment, though, because Ms. Sabatino said that she'd give me a chance to redo my project for a B (if I do a super-great job). She said I should stick to the original topic but could change all other elements of the experiment. And I don't even have to turn it in until the end of the semester, which is after the actual science fair, but all I really care about at this point is losing the F+! Ms. Sabatino is the coolest!

Wednesday, February 7
Sixth period

I like the way Chip laughs. When he laughs, it's not one of those breathy giggles or chuckles that only involves a person's mouth. Chip's laughter sounds like it comes from deep inside. Like his soul is happy. I couldn't help but notice this today because something really hilariously funny happened when Ms. Sabatino handed back my notebook with the earthworm project data.

Like I mentioned before, I designed my science project notebook to look almost *exactly* like my soul-mate project notebook. Of course I'd *hoped* something hilariously funny would happen, but usually I'm not so lucky.

Anyway, once the notebook was in my hands, I purposely left it on my desk and went to sharpen a pencil. Maybelline fell for it! Before I could get back to my seat, she'd grabbed it. "Aha!" she sneered. "*Now* we can see who you've been writing about in *Soul Observations.*"

Heads turned. I told her to give back the book—that it was my private property. This only encouraged her. (I knew it would!)

"It's not really *your* book because you have to be writing about us. What other souls do you know? Can't be many." She was whispering loudly, in an attempt to keep her voice low enough for Ms. Sabatino to pretend not to hear while watching YouTube science videos, but loud enough for everyone else to tune in.

I made a fake grab for the book, which prompted Maybelline to flip it open and start reading. "What?" she gasped. "This isn't about souls!"

"Right," I said. "It's about soils. You'd have known that if you read the cover carefully in the first place." I ripped the journal from her hands and held up it for the class to see. Maybelline looked shocked, then embarrassed. (Which is the first time I've ever seen *that* expression on her face.)

Then Chip about fell out of his chair laughing. Most people don't want to go head-to-head with Maybelline so no one else laughed out loud, but quite a few others were suddenly finding the tops of their desks awfully amusing. Chip didn't seem to care, though. He laughed so loudly that Ms. Sabatino was forced to stop pretending she didn't hear us and start a lesson, which wasn't the best part of the scenario.

Neither was the part where Maybelline's well-mascara'd eyelids narrowed and she hissed, "Is this the same book I saw the first time?"

I nodded. "I've been working on the earthworm project for some time."

She didn't look exactly like she believed me. But she didn't look exactly like she didn't, either. Mission accomplished.

Subject #5: CHIP TYLER (Card 2)

Data Collected on: 2/7   Status: Available

Hair: Improved. Has mousse in it or something

Eyes: Chocolate

Eyebrows: Insignificant

Body Type: Tallish

Age: 13 (Birthday last week)

Nice-o-meter: ☺☺☺☺☺

Interest Level: Really? Am I interested?

Observation: If laughter is a reflection of his soul, Chip's soul is happy!

After school

Well, the tables have turned and I'm not sure where my place is anymore. Because now instead of *me* seeking *him* out, Evan is seeking me out. No kidding. He came over and talked to me before school yesterday, and today he sat with me at lunch. Tabbi hadn't gotten to the cafeteria at that point, but when she arrived, she blew right by us. She and James went and sat near the windows instead.

If only Tabbi had broken up with Evan instead of the other way around! Because he's so nice (other than dumping Tabs) and so funny. I'm always laughing when he's around. I can't help it! But I wish I could, because I was laughing at something he said in the cafeteria when I looked up and caught Tabbi's eyes. At that particular moment, they looked like eyes that belonged in a face that had never laughed. Even her eyelashes looked angry. And she wouldn't answer my calls or my texts after school.

So I'm going to have to find somewhere to sit tomorrow where Evan won't find me. At this point in my life, I need a BFF more than I need a BF. And Tabbi's eyes told me that she's not over Evan yet, no matter what her mouth says.

End of discussion.

Bedtime

I can't help thinking about Chip laughing when Maybelline grabbed my notebook. I mean, was he doing that to impress me? He certainly didn't care about what Maybelline thought! Or did he just laugh because he thought it was funny? I thought it was hilarious myself. And I can't help thinking about Evan, either. Because when *I* sat with *him* at lunch, it was because I was interested in him. Does it work both ways? Could I, Kara McAllister, actually have two guys interested in me?

The Love-Bug Race: A Picture Chart
or
Amount of Interest Guys at My School Have Shown in Me
(Even If Some of Them Are Forever Off-Limits Due to BFF)
by Kara McAllister

START
(Barely notice me. Most guys stay right here)

AND THEY'RE OFF
(Notice me, but only as a friend)

IT'S NOSE TO NOSE
(Guys who are actually flirting with me . . . I think)

FINISH
(Who will win?)

Thursday, February 8
Fourth period

Today I had the chance to have my first (tiny!) conversation with Dylan Hudson. I guess I should say I *made* the chance by forcing myself to sit at Maybelline's table. I know. But I had to find a place where Evan wouldn't join me. And sitting next to Maybelline pretty much guaranteed that.

You should've seen her face when I walked over, by the way. She slowly looked me up and down and said, "What are *you* doing here, Scara?" So I told her that I'd been admiring her fingernails and I wondered if she could give me some tips to help me get mine looking better. (Dad claims that no one can resist talking about themselves. This must be true because even though she rolled her eyes and said, "As if," before I sat down, she didn't try to stop me and she immediately began talking about her nail-care regimen.)

Anyway, while I was there I was able to speak to Dylan a few times, giving him a chance to fire back one-word responses such as "Righteous" and "Hmmm." And, to be honest, he completely ignored a few of the things I said.

Which was probably some kind of karma because I was completely ignoring Evan when he walked by with his tray and lifted his eyebrows in a way that asked *Why the heck are you sitting there?* I have to admit that it hurt to see the look on his face — to feel that he wanted to be sitting with me and to know that I wanted to sit with him, too.

But I made the right decision. When I called Tabs after school, she answered.

Friday, February 9
After school

I had only been at my desk in English for a minute when I felt someone pull one of my curls. (Why can't I have straight hair?) I wheeled around with a dirty look already pasted on my face, thinking I was going to be aiming it at Maybelline. Unfortunately, that's who usually sits behind me.

"Whoa!" said Chip. He held up both hands. "I thought we were cool after being in detention together."

After assuring him that we "were cool" and explaining that it was a case of mistaken identity, I started having a really nice conversation with him. It began in the usual way . . . him telling me the new funny fake names he'd heard (Faye Slift, Lee Nover, Al B. Zienya). But then he saw that I was reading *Inkheart*, which is a book about a man who has a talent for *reading* characters out of books. Like, they actually come out of the books and interact with people. (*So* many times I wish I had that talent . . . only I wish I could *read* celebrities out of magazines instead.) Anyway, he got kind of excited when he saw *Inkheart* because he said it was one of his favorites. So we started discussing it. I didn't know you could have conversations like that with guys.

While we were talking, he twisted my hair around his finger and I could feel it gently tugging at my scalp and I can't explain why, but I think I liked it. For a millisecond I wondered what it would have been like if we *had* kissed in that closet.

Our discussion was completely ruined a few minutes later when The Vine walked over.

"What are you two talking about?" she asked.

"*Inkheart*," said Chip.

"Ooooo. That sounds really interesting." The Vine scooted behind Chip and started RUBBING HIS SHOULDERS like she was suddenly a massage therapist. She pretended to look interested while we talked about the book a little more. But really, the conversation had taken a nosedive because Chip didn't seem that interested anymore.

"So." I looked at The Vine. "Have you ever read *Inkheart*?"

"Nope." The Vine shook her black hair, then tugged at Chip's shirt. "Isn't it about time for class to start?" He let go of my hair and stood up. Then The Vine grabbed his arm and escorted him back to his seat as if he needed her help. I mean, it's not like he's an old lady who can't cross a street alone.

Now, I'm the first to admit that Chip is a total dweeb . . .

but I kind of wish he hadn't let The Vine get intertwined in our conversation. For the first time in my life I wished that Maybelline had been sitting in her usual place behind me.

Saturday, February 10
Early. Too early.

Just got off of the phone with Tabs, who apparently couldn't wait until a decent hour to call even though it is Saturday and sleeping in is about as much fun as I can expect to have on weekends at this point. It was not one of my favorite conversations.

Tabs: Kara? You were awake, weren't you?

Me: Mmmmm.

Tabs: Good! 'Cause I can't wait to tell you who James and I saw at the movies last night.

Me: Mmmmm.

Tabs: The Vine. And guess who she's creeping around now.

Me: (*Suddenly springing up even though I have a sinking feeling*) I'm not sure I wanna know.

Tabs: Of course you do. It's Chip.

Me:

Tabs: Can you believe that? Like, I know we give Gina a

hard time and all, but can you believe she likes that dork? I don't know what she sees in him.

(I do. But I didn't admit this to Tabbi.)

Me: Hmmm. Interesting.

Tabs: She was *all over* him, too.

Me: Um, you mind if I call you back? I was kinda asleep when you called and I'm having trouble concentrating.

Hopefully by the time I call Tabs back, she'll have something better to talk about. I don't want to hear about how Chip Tyler, who thought he was too good to get a perfectly-free-no-strings-attached-spin-the-bottle kiss from me, is now kissing The Vine. How humiliating for me. And for Chip. Why can't he see that he can do better?

Not that I like him! I totally don't. I just thought he was interested in me. But even if I *did* decide that I liked him at some point in the future, I could never go out with him now. He's off-limits FOREVER. Because how could I like a guy who lets The Vine hang all over him?

How will I ever find a soul mate when everyone keeps getting off-limits? I'll probably have to move to some more populated area. Like New York City. Or China. Some place where there are so many guys that The Vine wouldn't have time to get to them all.

And someone would be left for me.

After lunch

To: Kara M <Craftychick@mailquickly.com>
From: BebeTruelove <bebe@bebetruelove.com>
Subject: Tip #6

Dear Soul Mate Seeker,

Remember that your soul mate is that one person who shares your hopes and dreams. So he should share your interests as well. Find someone who shares your interests and maybe you've found someone to share your life.

Tip #6: Find common interests.

Good Luck in Love,

Bebe

TAKE AN INTEREST SURVEY!
NOT SURE WHAT YOU LIKE? TAKE OUR FREE INTEREST SURVEY
AND WE'LL TELL YOU MORE ABOUT YOURSELF. A FIVE DOLLAR
PROCESSING FEE WILL APPLY.
CLICK HERE TO TAKE SURVEY!
♥ INTEREST ♥
(MUST BE 18 YEARS OF AGE TO ORDER.)

Thanks a lot, Bebe. I thought I'd found common interests with Chip, but The Vine ruined it.

Sunday, February 11
After lunch

Furthering my soul mate search via my science project was almost the last thing I wanted to do after hearing about Chip and The Vine. Unfortunately, the *absolute last* thing I wanted to do was keep that F+ in the grade book. So I spent a good part of yesterday lying around on my fluffy white cloud rug gazing at my Christmas-light stars while trying to think of ways to get a larger sampling for my surveys. I really wanted to survey guys who don't go to my school because I'm pretty close to concluding that every guy there is a jerk, a jock, or has dated The Vine.

I thought about handing out the surveys at the mall or something. But that'd probably make me look pretty desperate. Then I thought I could do one of those phone surveys. I'd dial random numbers, ask if there was a teenager in the house, and conduct the survey. But I remembered how many times I've hung up on people giving phone surveys. Finally, I thought of the perfect place to distribute tons of surveys anonymously. It's that alternate social networking universe where enemies are friends, friends are friends, strangers are friends, and relationships have nothing to do with reality. Faceplace.

After logging into my FP account at the "family computer located in a high-traffic area," I typed *surveys* into the search bar. Not a ton of stuff came up. But when I typed in *quizzes* . . . well, let's just say that's the buzzword! I found out there are over a million FP quizzes already. And that quizzes help you "find your social identity." Perfect. After all, a quiz is just a survey where the results only matter to one person. Once I compile all of the data I gather from my quiz it will morph into a survey!

In the interest of research, I took a few of the FP quizzes. Here are the results.

Survey Title:	Result:
What Kind of Food Are You?	Carrot (Great. I'm a root.)
What Occupation Will You Have?	Data Analyst, Teacher (Wow. Exciting.)
Which Cartoon Character Are You?	Velma (!)

I guess if I wear thick Velma glasses with orange mini-skirts and turtlenecks when I grow up, it isn't too much of a stretch to say I'll be a data analyst, a teacher, or a carrot. Even though I don't want to think my destiny has been decided, maybe there is something to these quizzes. I don't know. They were awfully short. Short and witty. So I made some major changes to my original surveys. I tried to make

Dude! Take this crushin' crush quiz!

(Ages 12–16 only.)

Questions

1. A girl's gotta like what I like.

- ○ Totally!
- ○ Hey, she's gotta like some of the same stuff.
- ○ Not!

2. A chick's looks are all that.

- ○ Totally!
- ○ Hey, she's gotta try, man.
- ○ Not!

3. I like it when a girl lets me know she's into me.

- ○ Totally!
- ○ Hey, flirting never hurts.
- ○ Not! She should B hard 2 get!

4. Self–confident chicks are hot.

- ○ Totally!
- ○ Yep. But there has 2 B room for my ego, too.
- ○ Not!

5. When it comes to girls, I'm looking for

- ○ A good time!
- ○ Someone to go out with.
- ○ My 1 and only soul mate.

the wording hip, so kids would want to take them.

This time I made the girls' quiz just like the guys', except I changed the *she*s to *he*s and all. And, since Ms. S said I could change the experiment as long as I stuck to the same general topic, I formed new hypotheses, too.

#1: Official Science Fair Hypothesis

I think interest surveys will show that male and female teens are looking for different things in relationships.

AND

#2: Hidden Agenda Project Hypothesis

Finding out what boys are looking for will help me discover how to find my soul mate!

Is there is a better way to figure out what guys like than to ask them directly? I don't think so! They don't call this kind of feedback a primary source for nothing!

When I finished filling out my new science fair application with my new and improved hypothesis, I brought Julie and Tabbi in on my plan. They promised to get James and Lyle to take the guy version. Now I just have to sit back and see how far the ball rolls. . . .

```
        WEEK 6: RESEARCH REVIEW
   # of subjects unobtrusively studied: 1

Most significant finding: Chip Tyler can't be
my soul mate. Subject was observed by a third
             party with The Vine.

            New Research Strategy:
      Send out survey to a wider audience!

Bebe Truelove's Tip #6: Find common interests.

    Data Collection Methods: observation,
            Faceplace quizzes
```

Monday, February 12
Lunch

Chip, who is partially hidden by his hugging GF, is waving at me across the lunchroom. I'm not waving back.

Fifth period

We were watching a YouTube video of some science experiment when one of those paper footballs landed on my desk. I was about to brush it to the floor when I saw my name on it. So I unfolded it. It was a note from Evan. He'd written three words: *Can we talk?*

Six months ago, I'd have given anything to get a note from Evan. Not now.

Tuesday, February 13
Lunch

Chip sat in Maybelline's seat in English today. He probably wouldn't have done it if The Vine hadn't been absent. He tugged my hair but I didn't turn around. He said, "Hey, we never finished talking about *Inkheart*." Doesn't he realize that I'm acutely (new vocab word) aware of the specific reason we didn't get to finish that conversation?

So I told him I'd moved on to other books. To prove my point, I opened *Cross My Heart and Hope to Spy*, which is a book about a girl who goes to an all-girl spy school where you can't have boyfriends, but somehow *she* still manages to get one. I heard him get up and go back to his seat.

Wednesday, February 14
Lunch. In the boys' room. Again. Really.

I'm sitting here stranded, once again, in my private office

cubicle. That's right. The last stall in the boys' room. What a romantic place to spend lunch on Valentine's Day. This probably tops the list of "Stupid Things Kara Has Done." At least last time I was kind of forced in here by survival instinct. I had to flee Maybelline. I was lucky to escape then with no one seeing me. Why did I risk possible detention and definite humiliation again?

Actually, I know why. But knowing something is a lot easier than forcing yourself to admit it to someone else. See, I heard Chip tell The Vine he'd meet her at lunch after he used the restroom. Then, without really thinking about what I was doing, I ran in here ahead of him and locked myself in my now favorite stall. I guess I thought I'd hear him tell someone *something* while he was in here that would clue me in on how serious he is about The Vine. WHY DO I CARE?

Anyway, my plan totally backfired because not only has Chip failed to come in and start revealing information, Jonah Nate has not. I can tell it's him because he's talking about the Civil War. What other middle school boy uses lunch period to do that? He has poor Richie Lopez, whose accent gives him away, cornered as he rambles on and on. I can't leave unless they leave first, obviously.

Wait . . . I just heard my name. They're talking about *ME*!!!!! I'm writing this down.

Richie: Really? You think Kara likes you? (What? Surely he's talking about some other Kara.)

Jonah Nate: She *begged* to borrow one of my Civil War books. (Okay, it has to be me. But I NEVER begged. Asked. Did NOT beg.)

Richie: Oh? (Sounds surprised. I admit, it is pretty surprising.)

Jonah Nate: Yeah. I think she wanted to sleep with it under her pillow. (EWW and YUCK!)

Sound Effect: Door opens. Guys grunt greeting to each other. Can't tell who entered. Water in sink is running.

Jonah Nate: Anyway, since I'm pretty sure Kara likes me, I'm thinking about asking her to the spring dance. (!)

Person who just entered: Kara McAllister?

Jonah Nate: Yeah.

Person: Dude, Kara is *way* out of your league. (True! But I feel flattered to hear someone else say it. Could it be Chip? Oh, to be a fly on the wall instead of a girl in a stall!)

Jonah Nate: Shut up, Chip! (It *is* Chip!)

Chip: Whatever.

Sound Effect: Feet leaving.

Jonah Nate: He's jealous.

Richie: No, man. He has a pretty girl already. Gina. (*Cringe!*)

Jonah Nate: She's not as pretty as Kara. (At least he's got good taste.)

There's no point writing down the rest of what they said, because the discussion went right back to the Civil War. *Blah*

blah blah Civil War relics. *Blah blah* metal detectors. *Blah* fifteen and a half rusting musket balls. It was a pretty one-sided conversation, of course, with Jonah Nate doing most of the talking, but I'm pretty sure Richie was nodding his head. And smiling.

I just looked at my watch. Richie and Jonah Nate have spent almost the entire lunch period hanging out in the boys' room. Who does that? Besides me, I mean.

Why—won't—they—leave? Leave! Please leave! Please do not wait until the bell rings to walk out of that door.

They're still talking. I am *so* going to be tardy. . . .

Fourth period

Tardy. Definitely tardy. But that's not the worst bathroom-related thing that happened to me today. Not even close. See, as soon as I heard the door shut behind Jonah Nate and Richie, I made a break for it. But just as I stepped out of the stall, someone stepped into the bathroom. And it was Evan, of all people.

I had been ignoring Evan for the past two days, but it's hard to ignore a guy when he's the only other person in the room.

"Kara!" he said, looking surprised. Shocked, actually. "What are you *doing* in here?"

I didn't say anything.

He smiled that gorgeous smile and walked toward me.

I couldn't get my feet to move.

The bell started ringing.

I still couldn't get my feet to move.

"Why didn't you answer my note?"

Bell still ringing. Me still not speaking. What could I say?

"You know," he said, moving even closer, "I think I picked the wrong one." Then he leaned forward and kissed me. My first kiss!

I may never be able to forgive Evan for it either. Because he ruined it. You only get one first kiss and when that happens, you are supposed to be able to:

(a) tell your best friend about it.

(b) always remember exactly where it happened.

And thanks to Evan, these are the sensory experiences that I will forever associate with that moment.

SIGHT: urinal

SMELL: you don't want to know

TASTE: peanut butter

TOUCH: too panicked to enjoy

SOUND: bell ringing like some sort of cosmic alarm — letting me know I was going to be in trouble *no matter what*

Finally both my voice and feet started working. I squeaked something that sounded a lot like "EEEP!" and bolted. Which ended up being the worst possible thing I could have done, because I was so panicked about the whole situation that I forgot to peek around the door before running out into the hall. So I ran smack into Maybelline, who's always going to class at the last chime of the bell.

Maybelline looked at me, then at the pants-wearing figure on the door I'd just exited. She said one word: "Freak." But I knew she'd have a lot more to say to a lot more people, and soon.

Fifth period

Geez, it's only been an hour since I arrived in fourth period (tardy). But when we were changing classes just now, Dylan Hudson—who has barely ever spoken to me besides the time I sat at Maybelline's lunch table—pointed right at me and yelled, "Hey! There's Peeping Thomasina!" (Peeping Thomasina! They think I was trying to look! Which is totally creepy. My reputation is ruined!)

Maybelline never showed up for algebra. She obviously roamed the halls broadcasting what she saw, which I hope didn't include Evan leaving the restroom right after me! It's bad enough that she saw *me* come out of those doors, but if she knew I'd been in there with a guy . . . and that I'd kissed him . . . (even if I hadn't meant to) . . . I may as well pack up and move to Alaska, because I'll be a permanent outcast without even a best friend to stand by me. Because the last place Tabs will stand if she finds out about me and Evan is anywhere near me.

Almost as soon as I got to science, a note from Tabbi landed on my desk.

What were you doing in the boys' room?

I didn't write back. But I was relieved. The note didn't say a word about Evan. Still, I avoided Tabs for the rest of the day.

My afternoon was miserable with worrying that everyone will think I'm a total weirdo. I wish I could tell Tabbi the real reason I went in there but, well, admitting something to yourself is a lot easier than admitting something to anyone else.

As far as Dylan Hudson goes, I think he must have a major character flaw if he feels like it's okay to yell something rude across a crowded hallway to someone he never usually bothers to speak to. I mean, he was already down pretty low on my list of possibilities, but now I know there is no further research needed on Subject #14.

Subject #14: DYLAN HUDSON (Card 2)
Data Collected on: 2/14   Status: Never available for
Hair: Thick, gorgeous, blondish   more than ½ a day
Eyes: Dark brown
Eyebrows: Perfect, but not worth it
Body Type: See "Eyebrows"
Age: 13
Nice-o-meter: -1000
Interest Level: zip, zero, nada, nothing

After school

How ironic is it that my realization that I'll never, ever find a soul mate, or even a boyfriend, occurs on Valentine's Day! All this research has done is wreck my life. As of today I am giving up this stupid research project!

THE SCIENTIFIC METHOD

Step 3: Construct a Hypothesis

My Hypothesis:
Trying to Find a Soul Mate Is a
Stupid Waste of Time!

THE SCIENTIFIC METHOD

Step 4: Experiment. Test Your Hypothesis.

My life before the soul mate research project:

Good Things
science grade
no detentions
hadn't kissed BFF's ex
reputation

Bad Things
no boyfriend

My life after the soul mate research project:

Good Things

Bad Things
science grade
detentions
kissed BFF's ex
reputation

And still no boyfriend!

These charts pretty much prove that my research project is a complete and total failure. It's a terrible thing to devote your life to science and come up empty-handed.

Thursday, February 15
Before school

I feel sick. I woke up with the word *freak* bouncing around in my head. As it boinged from one side of my brain to the other, the word sounded just like it did when it exited Maybelline's mouth and journeyed down my ear canal. "Freak."

How can I face my friends when they think I'm a Peeping Tom? Or something else. Something so bad that I can't make myself write it.

And how can I face Tabbi? Because even though I didn't kiss Evan back yesterday . . . I wanted to. It feels like I drank a concrete milk shake and my insides are turning hard and heavy.

Third period (Except I'm at home, not in class)

I told Mom my stomach hurt too bad to go to school. She believed me after I downed a dose of Pepto-Bismol, because she knows I hate the stuff. (I do. But unfortunately, there are worse things in life than Pepto-Bismol.)

Normally I'd celebrate a free day off but I'm pretty weepy. I know Mom's concerned, but I just can't make myself tell her the real reason I'm feeling sick. ☹ I don't want her to be disappointed in me and I don't think she'd understand.

After school

My cell is ringing, but I'm not even going to look at who's calling. What's the use? I don't plan on talking to anyone EVER AGAIN. I'm a humiliation hermit.

After Julie's track practice, which is some point between the end of school and the beginning of dinner

Thanks to Julie's skill at using a paper clip to open locked doors (worthless privacy locks!), I was only able to maintain hermit status for a few hours. Julie forced herself into my room, then forced me into a conversation. She started with, "Phillip told Lyle what people are saying."

This is apparently one of those phrases that trigger those terrible sobs. The type that causes burning in the space between your lungs so that it feels like you've been seared on the inside. I guess a good thing about being human is that you can only cry like that for so long, no matter how bad you feel.

Eventually, I spilled the whole story about my *Soul Observations* notebook and how I was doing research and how I'd accidentally discovered that hiding in the boys' room was a great way to gather data. And I told her that I was worried that I was never going to find a soul mate. Especially now that I'm a social outcast and labeled a Peeping Thomasina.

"Look," said Julie. "I know it doesn't seem like it, but the rumors will pass. Promise."

"What are the rumors exactly?" I sniffed.

Julie winced. "Colleen is telling everyone that you were spying on the boys."

Okay, maybe you *can* cry the inside-searing cry for all eternity. Maybe at some point when you burst into tears, you simultaneously burst into flames. I think I'd have been okay with that.

Julie put her arm around me. "Phillip doesn't believe that. He said Colleen was really mean. That's why he told Lyle. Lyle doesn't believe it either. That's why he told me. They're worried about you. Just tell anyone who asks that you really, really had to go. Say it was an emergency and that you couldn't make it all the way to the other end of the hall."

Then I told Julie about the thing — the heavy thing — that was really bothering me. I told her about what had happened with Evan. She said no one had mentioned Evan, which was good. But she also said, "You're going to have to tell Tabbi about the kiss. You know that, right?" Which was bad, but true. I don't have the energy to do it today, though.

Never Mind: A Statement
by Kara McAllister

I guess I won't give up my research project after all. Because Julie said she'd take me to the mall to cheer me up, and then I remembered something. I mean, someone. (Subject #11: AKA Guy at the Mall)

Friday, February 16
After dinner

Julie thought more days at home would help my situation because then it will be the weekend and then it'll be Presidents' Day, so that'll give everyone five whole days to forget about the whole bathroom incident.

The only downside to this plan is the Pepto-Bismol. And knowing that I'm worrying Mom.

While I was sitting around at home today I made two charts.

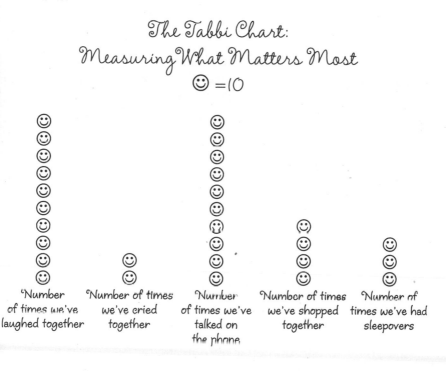

The Tabbi Chart:
Measuring What Matters Most
☺ = 10

Number of times we've laughed together

Number of times we've cried together

Number of times we've talked on the phone

Number of times we've shopped together

Number of times we've had sleepovers

The Evan Chart:
Measuring What Matters Most
☺ = 10

☺

| Number of times we've laughed together | Number of times we've cried together | Number of times we've talked on the phone | Number of times we've shopped together | Number of times we've had sleepovers |

Pretty Bleak!

When I think about all of the time Tabs and I have spent together, here is what I *can't* imagine: life without Tabbi. I've had my best times with her.

But here is what I *can* imagine: life without Evan. Basically, all I have to do is look back on my life to date.

I can't say for one hundred percent sure that Evan is *not* going to end up being my soul mate. You never know. Years from now, things might be different. But today I can't even imagine what school would be like if Tabbi weren't my friend. So I called her. She came over and I told her about Evan kissing me. (I couldn't bring myself to tell her about my crush on him. It doesn't matter anyway because I'm making him one hundred percent off-limits. I mean it this time!)

Tabbi wasn't mad at me. More like sad. Which made me sad. And she said some crazy things like, "Do you think he tried to kiss you because he knew you would tell me and then I'd be jealous?"

And even though I know she was hurting inside, she promised to stand by me with the really-really-had-to-go story. Like I said, one of the best things about Tabbi is that she's loyal. And I'm going to be loyal to her, too. If that gets in the way of me finding a soul mate . . . well, that's okay.

Bedtime

Went to the "family computer located in a high-traffic area" to check out my FP survey and guess what: 146 chicks and 89 dudes have responded! So far, I like what I see. Most guys don't seem to think a girl's looks are *totally* important and they like confident girls. . . . Hmmm.

Even fewer girls cared about looks, but this didn't surprise me. They like confidence too, though!

Saturday, February 17
On the way to the mall

Ever since Julie offered to take me to the mall—and I remembered who worked there—I can't stop thinking about him. His gorgeous eyes framed by gorgeous eyebrows are vivid in my memory. I can almost feel the way he touched my arm. What if he's "the one"? I know I don't know him, but last night I started wondering if what I am feeling toward JUSTIN is *Love at First Sight*.

What? It happens! I did some research on it last night and discovered that not only is ♥ @ 1st *sigh*+t a real phenomenon, but there are three characteristics that prove you have a case of it. Guess what. I have all three.

Here they are:

1. You are attracted to the way the person looks, but also recognize some other quality. (He's super-cute. But I think that tingly feeling was the other quality.)

2. You can't stop thinking about him. (I've been experimenting with name morphs like everyone makes for celebrities. My favorite is Justin + Kara = Jara)

3. You want to learn everything there is to know about him. (Do I ever!)

So it seems pretty obvious that this is ♥ @ 1st *sigh*+t. I only have one problem. I'll die if he recognizes me as the girl who asked about him, then ran out of the store pulling her mother behind her. Good thing I have Julie to help me accessorize!

On the way home from the mall

When I walked through the doors at A&F, JUSTIN didn't seem to recognize me at all. Okay, so I had Julie do my hair and makeup, and lend me her boots. I guess I didn't exactly look like myself—I looked better. Older. More confident! Still. I think he should have been able to recognize me *a little bit* if I was supposed to be his soul mate. He'd have said something like "You look familiar." I mean the whole point of ♥ @ 1st *sigh*+t is that you fall for someone by just seeing them. But JUSTIN barely even looked at me because he was so busy looking at *her*. *Chicken Girl*.

I could tell by her uniform that she worked at the Chicken Hut in the food court. Plus, she smelled like drumstick. Anyway, at first I hung around and checked out the new tops and shorts. I tried to look confused, like I needed help. I even sighed loudly, which is universal shoppers' language for *I'm frustrated because I can't find what I need*. JUSTIN didn't seem to notice. He was leaning against the wall mirror (imagine two gorgeous JUSTINs in the same room) and he had his hand on *Chicken Girl's* arm. The same hand that gave me that tingly feeling and let me know (after I remembered it) that I was experiencing ♥ @ 1st *sigh*+t!

And the whole time I'd been in there, Chicken Girl hadn't looked at a single piece of clothing! She was only looking at *him*. Didn't she *know* he had customers who needed him?

When I realized that I only had five minutes left before I had to meet Julie, I cleared my throat and said—very politely—"Can you help me?"

Justin and Chicken Girl just stared at me. Then *she* answered instead of him. "He's helping *me* now," she said. She yanked a shirt off the rack, headed to the dressing room, and said, "C'mon, Justin. I need some help."

He shrugged at me. "Sorry, kid, but she was here first." *Kid!* And then he FOLLOWED HER!

I think it's pretty obvious now that I was mistaken about the ♥ @ 1st *sigh*+t thing. Justin can't possibly be my soul mate because now I can never go to A&F again and that was my favorite store and I'm pretty sure that your soul mate shouldn't keep you away from the things you love.

Subject Number #11: GUY AT THE MALL (Card 2)
AKA Justin (according to his plastic name tag)
New Data Collected on: 2/17   Status: Who cares?
Hair: Somehow, not as cool
Eyes: Needs glasses
Eyebrows: Still gorgeous. I have to give him that one.
Body Type: Ditto
Age: Still don't know
Fast Fact: ♥ @ 1st *sigh*+t is an illusion!

Sunday, February 18
Morning

Oddly, I actually believe Bebe's advice this time. For good reason.

To: Kara M <Craftychick@mailquickly.com>

From: BebeTruelove <bebe@bebetruelove.com>

Subject: Tip #7

Dear Soul Mate Seeker,

Body language is the language of love. A guy will direct his feet toward someone who interests him.

Tip #7: Try the foot test.

Good Luck in Love,

Bebe

See, this has to be true. It was pretty clear which direction Justin's feet were pointing when he was walking behind Chicken Girl—and away from me.

I'm not even doing a research review card for this week. What's the point?

Monday, February 19
Noonish

It'd be so much easier to face everyone at school tomorrow if it had turned out that Justin was my soul mate.

I mean, everyone could be like: "You're gross for hanging in the boys' room."

So I could be like: "My hot boyfriend doesn't think so."

Because even though I don't care at all what the kids at my school think about me, I really do.

Bedtime

I have the best sister ever! Julie just convinced me that everything is going to be okay.

"You just need to stick to the really-really-had-to-go (RRHTG) story, Kara," she said. "And act self-confident, like it's no big deal."

She walked over to her dresser and picked up a cute pair of pink-tinted sunglasses. "Here." She handed them to me. "Think of these as *shades of power.*"

"What of what?"

"Shades of power," she said. "See, it's your eyes that give away how you really feel."

"Proof that eyes are windows to the soul!" I exclaimed.

"Whatever," said Julie. "The point is that if Colleen can't see your eyes completely, she can't get to you completely. If she thinks you're self-confident, she'll probably leave you alone."

I put on the sunglasses. "It's like I'll have my own personal soul shields."

"Like I said." Julie flipped her ponytail. (I hate when she does that, but she's still pretty great.) "Whatever."

"You're the best, Julie," I said.

My sister got a funny look on her face for a second. Then she gave me one of her super-quick hugs. "You are, too."

Spring Valley Middle, are you ready for this? The new Kara McAllister is about to come back to campus packing an attitude and cute shades!

Tuesday, February 20
First period

Last night, everything Julie said made so much sense. But if I'd thought about what it'd be like to step out of the car at 7:15 a.m. wearing sunglasses I'd have known

Cute Shades @ Beach = Cool

BUT

Cute Shades B4 Sunrise = Loser

Once I realized this, I didn't feel very powerful. I felt more like I wanted to run. And I wished I hadn't given up my morning jogs with Julie because if I hadn't, maybe I'd have been fast enough to actually escape the entire day.

But I wouldn't have had a chance to make a clean getaway anyway because Tabbi grabbed me, dragged me into the building, and pulled me toward our lockers. I was still wearing the "shades of power" but I couldn't make myself look up.

Unfortunately, walking with your head down in a crowded hallway is one way to *guarantee* that you'll *absolutely positively* have to look up because eventually you're going to bump smack into someone, which is what I did to Evan. And when you bump into someone . . . you automatically look up.

"Hi, Tabbi. Hi, Kara," said Evan, all cheerful-like. "I miss hanging out with you guys. We should do something together sometime." (!) Like he hadn't secretly kissed me or broken Tabs's heart.

I stood vthere, my own heart beating wildly while my tongue lay dead as a canned sardine in my mouth. Tabbi broke the silence by barking, "I don't think *James* would like that very much."

Evan raised his eyebrows before saying, "Right." Then he smiled, waved, and merged back into the crowd.

"Can you believe that jerk?" asked Tabbi. But she turned around and watched him go all the way down the hall before she started walking again. This let me know that even after everything—she'd take him back. Tabs's feelings for Evan are the real thing.

Watching her, I knew I didn't feel that deeply toward him. Maybe I never really did.

After school

Sometimes girls hunt in packs. Like wolves. They single out a weaker animal and work together to bring it down. We learned about this last year in science. And I learned about it firsthand in English today. I am the hunted.

I knew that Maybelline would go for the jugular the first chance she got. Which was about ten minutes into Mrs. Hill's class. But she didn't do it alone. First The Sponge asked for a bathroom pass. Mrs. Hill handed it to her without even pausing during her lecture on *When Zachary Beaver Came to Town*, which is a book about someone who has almost *no* chance of finding his soul mate because he lives in a tiny trailer that he almost never leaves.

About thirty seconds later, Maybelline asked for a bathroom pass. This brought the lecture to a screeching halt.

"Colleen!" snapped Mrs. Hill. "You know I don't give out more than one girls' room pass at a time!"

"Yes, I know," said Maybelline in a sweet voice as fake as her nail color. "But I have to go really bad. And I heard that it's okay for girls to go into the boys' room if they really, really have to go. Kara did it."

The class broke into hyena-pitched hysterics. I could feel my skin morphing strawberry red. And I swear I could sense Maybelline's smile spread across her face to watermelon-slice proportions.

Mrs. Hill gave Maybelline a sharp look. She rapped her pen against the podium. "Quiet!" she barked about three times before yelling words that will somber any mood: "Pop Quiz!"

"This is all *your* fault," hissed Maybelline. She "accidentally" shoved my desk while putting away her book.

About that time, The Sponge came bopping into the room, smiling smugly. "Sorry I was gone so long, Mrs. Hill. I hope no one else *really, really had to go.*" She glanced knowingly at Maybelline, whose face must have looked like the face of a kid whose teacher just yelled "Pop Quiz" because The Sponge's smile faded and she hurried to her seat.

When the bell rang I rushed from class, even though there was nowhere for me to hide this time. Maybelline was sure to go to the girls' room with her posse, and the boys' room is now forever off-limits. So I decided to sit at my usual lunch table and hope that some of my friends still liked me enough to join me.

With no one to talk to I tried to look absorbed in my PB&J, but I saw Chip take a seat just one table away. Unfortunately, The Vine walked over and slung an arm around his shoulder. She leaned close to his ear like she was going to tell him a secret, then whispered VERY LOUDLY, "I wish Mrs. Hill had written Kara up when Colleen spilled her nasty little secret. She'd deserve it. The perv."

Chip abruptly stood up, causing The Vine's arm to fall against her side. Before he walked away he said, "Tell it to someone else, Gina. Kara's my friend."

The look on The Vine's face was *almost* worth all of the humiliation I've endured. I couldn't tell if Chip knew I was within hearing distance or not, but it doesn't matter. Because now I know that someone besides my sister and my best friend will stick up for me, which gives me hope that other people will, too. Know what? Having hope makes you feel a whole lot more powerful than wearing "shades of power." (No matter how cute those shades may be.)

Wednesday, February 21
First period

When I was entering the building this morning, I passed Alex Brantley. He said, "'Morning, Kara," which is actually remarkable because he usually only gives me a halfway smile. But this time he smiled big AND he looked at me in a different way. I know I wasn't imagining it. Sure, maybe it's still a *little bit* the way he would look at a dictionary. But I think he sees a piece of gum sitting on top of it now.

Sixth period

This really cute eighth grader who I don't even know stopped me in the cafeteria and said, "Aren't you Kara McAllister?"

When I nodded he said, "Cool." What gives?

After school

James bent over backward to talk to me in band, which seemed weird because we hardly ever talk even though he's going out with my best friend. Tabbi later told me that James told *her* that the guys thought it was cool that I had the guts to use their restroom.

So I remain silently horrified, even though I'm also secretly excited that the guys think I did something "cool." Maybe nothing bad will come of this. Maybe Julie is right. Maybe it will all blow over. Maybe it has already blown over.

Thursday, February 22
Fourth period

It has not blown over. I hadn't counted on the creative way that Maybelline and her pack would find to torture me.

So I was totally surprised when I headed to my seat in algebra and there was a big Depend undergarment resting in it like a fluffy white cushion! The giant diaper had a huge gift tag hanging on it that could be read from, like, a mile away. It said: *To Kara. Next time you really, really have to go, you won't have to do it in the boys' room.*

I probably stood there for a good forty seconds while panic set in and I tried to calculate how many people read the tag before I did. Then I kicked into übergear and started stuffing the white elephant into my backpack. If I'd been in a TV sitcom instead of a classroom, there'd have been the kind of laughter in the background that sounds like it's coming from the far end of a long tunnel. I know this because that's what it sounded like to me. In reality, though, the snickers and guffaws were blasting from the surrounding desks.

Then Mr. DeLacey walked up and asked, "What are you doing, Kara?" I told him I was just putting something away. He wasn't satisfied with this answer. He held out his hand in a way that means *hand it over* in teacher sign language.

I don't know what Mr. DeLacey thought I was going to put in his hand, but it sure wasn't a giant diaper. I swear he almost dropped it. Then he read the tag, went to his desk, and got out a referral slip. The class was now hushed with somebody's-gonna-get-it silence. Mr. DeLacey's face was very serious, and while I watched him, I found it hard to believe that I'd ever found him handsome.

I heard Maybelline catch her breath and I bet for a moment she thought *she* was going to get in trouble. But life is never that fair. Instead, Mr. DeLacey waved the referral slip in the air and said, "Kara." So I grabbed my backpack and the slip and left the room, knowing this was his way of getting me back for the "Is it legal for you to . . ." question that I wish my dad had never taught me to use.

I waited until I was here, outside of Principal O'Neal's

office, to look at it. I'm glad I did because I'm working very hard not to cry as I stare at the words: *Office Referral. First offense. Girl found in boys' restroom.*

So now the slowest minutes of my life are crawling by while I wait for Mr. O'Neal to finish his conference call. Oddly, there are some painfully slow things that you still don't want to rush. I hope Mr. O'Neal talks a long, long time. Like, until the dismissal bell rings . . .

On the way home from school in the backseat of the car, where the only noise is the sound of me sniffing as I try to pull the tears back inside of me

Nothing says surrender like walking into the principal's office carrying a white flag in the shape of a giant diaper. I was surrendering my pride. Surrendering my dignity. Even worse, I was surrendering to Maybelline because this time she got what she wanted. She won.

Mr. O'Neal, who's usually pretty nice, looked at the diaper and took the referral slip. Then he asked, "Is this true, Kara?"

I hung my head and admitted that it was. I gave him my really-really-had-to go story. By the time I finished telling it, I was crying. He handed me the phone and told me to get one of my parents to pick me up. I thought this meant I was suspended, which is why I started crying even harder when I heard Dad's voice.

Without asking any questions or waiting to see what I needed, my dad said, "I'll be right there." And he was. Just a few minutes later. And I realized that the reason Dad didn't ask any questions is because the answer didn't matter. Dad was going to be there no matter what. Just like he has always been.

After school

My parents were super-understanding when I told them about the whole boys'-room fiasco. I pretty much cried my way through the story, especially at the end when I predicted that I'd have 0 friends left if I ever did get the nerve to go back to school.

Mom and Dad assured me that my prediction would be false. Then they both hugged me at the same time, which is something we used to call the "family group hug," but need to rename because Julie flatly refuses to participate anymore. (To tell you the truth, I thought I'd outgrown them too, but it turns out I haven't. ☺)

Anyway, Mom said for me to remember that regardless of what happened between me and my friends, she and Dad would "always be there" for me. I started thinking . . . that's a pretty important quality to have in a person: someone who will always be there for you. Like my parents are there for each other. And for me and Julie.

I need to add that quality to my soul mate list.

Another thing I need to add to my list is compassion. Which is something Mr. O'Neal has. I know this because Dad told me later that Mr. O'Neal did NOT send me home as a punishment. He just thought I needed to get away from whoever had left me the Depend. So I wasn't suspended after all. But I was embarrassed. Because Mr. O'Neal also told Dad to ask me to "plan ahead and pace myself by going to the appropriate facility throughout the day so that this will never happen again."

The Perfect Soul Mate: A List Revised
by Kara McAllister

My one and only soul mate will

1. be a nice person.
2. have a sense of humor.
3. like to read.
4. appreciate art.
5. think I'm great.
6. not teach algebra.
7. have never dated The Vine.
8. have compassion.
9. always be there.

Bedtime. Finally. It has been the longest day of my life. (But I feel better now.)

I guess I still looked pretty depressed during dinner, so Mom came to my room afterward. She sat on my bed and gave me the usual pep talk. It started with "Kara, you're better than that Colleen" and ended with "When life gives you lemons, make lemonade."

Of course, making lemonade out of lemons is not all that hard. But what are you supposed to do when life gives you a big white adult-size diaper?

This was the question I pondered (new vocab word) after Mom left and I lay on my bed staring at the Depend diaper on my desk. And then it hit me. I never should have tried to stuff that thing in my book bag! I never should have acted ashamed, because shame is what girls like Maybelline feed on!

Suddenly, I knew what to do. I combined Mom's "make lemonade" advice with her "a little fringe can dress up anything" philosophy. I grabbed the Depend and headed down to Mom's craft corner.

Knowing that duct tape is, like, the strongest substance on earth and that people use it to make everything from baseball caps to miniskirts, I figured I could use it to transform the Depend underwear into something cool. (Actually, the strongest thing on earth is a spiderweb or something crazy like that. We learned it in science, but I forgot the details after the test.)

Two hours later, I had created what I now call the Gotta-Go-on-the-Go Bag. It has a black and red braided duct-tape handle, black duct-tape fringe across the bottom, and a red duct-tape flap over the top. The only clue that my stylin' new bag was once a garment at the very bottom of the fashion food chain is a wide swath of the white Depend material that I left visible in the front center. I did this to show that I AM NOT ASHAMED!

Friday, February 23
Sixth period

"Cool bag," said Tabbi when I walked onto campus. Then she did what she always does when I get something new. She snatched it and started examining it as if it were hers.

"Wait," she said, running her hand over the white patch in front. "You didn't."

I nodded.

Then Tabbi laughed. Really loudly. She grabbed James's arm and doubled over.

James asked, "What's so funny, babe?" *Babe!* Cringe! But he laughed, too, when Tabs finally spit it out.

In the end a little group formed around me, which I'm sure shocked Maybelline. The Gotta-Go Bag was passed around and everyone seemed to like it.

Anna Johnstone even suggested I start a crafts blog!

"You totally should," agreed Tabbi. "You're so good with crafts! Remember that bracelet you made out of game pieces? You can transform any old thing into something beautiful!"

Hmmm. Maybe I *should* start a blog. If I'm willing to show the school that I AM NOT ASHAMED, why not show the world?

When Tabbi finished laughing, which was after the bell rang, BTW, she asked me to make her a bag, too. She says she'll carry it to show her support! Even better, on the way out of band, Malcolm (who I thought was off-limits forever) said, "Cool bag. Where'd you get it?"

When I told him I'd made it, he said he'd pay me to make him a backpack out of duct tape!

The fact that Malcolm actually noticed my handiwork makes me wonder if I misjudged him earlier. Maybe he was just joking about the gum wrapper. Maybe he had some wadded-up tissues in his pocket at the time. Maybe guys just think stuff like that is funny. Hmmm. How can I figure this out?

After school

Lyle was hanging out at our house watching TV in the basement with Julie this afternoon, and he saw me over in Mom's craft corner making the duct-tape backpack for Malcolm. He left Julie sitting on the sofa, walked over, and picked up the pack. "The way you've woven the black and silver tape together is cool," he said. "It looks like a chessboard. What else can you make?"

"Almost anything," I said. "When I was looking for backpack patterns, I saw all kinds of stuff—wallets, hammocks, and even prom dresses made out of duct tape. Malcolm Maxwell is paying me to make this pack."

Julie turned off the TV and joined us. "Ooooh. How much are you gonna charge?" she asked. "I'd ask at least thirty bucks. You can't buy anything good for less than thirty."

"How much for a wallet, Kara?" asked Lyle.

"I could probably do two of those for thirty dollars, since they don't use much tape."

"Sold," said Lyle. "One for me and one for Phillip."

When they were heading upstairs, I heard Lyle say, "Your kid sister is pretty cool."

Cha-ching! Two sales in one day. Even better—one of the cutest boys in town just called me "pretty cool." I don't care if he is dating my sister. It's still a massive compliment.

You know, Lyle is so nice. And Julie is so happy. I really hope that Lyle is Julie's one and only true soul mate! He'd make a great brother-in-law.

So I may not have found a soul mate yet, but at least I

found out what to do when life hands you a giant diaper: cover it with duct tape and sell it for thirty bucks!

Saturday, February 24
Afternoon

Being the BFF of someone with a BF and the sister of someone with a BF and even the enemy of someone with a BF, I found myself alone again on the weekend. Big surprise. I was moping around about it, too. You know, sighing and shutting doors loudly in a way that says, *Somebody ask me what's wrong, but if you do, I'm going to say "nothing" until you ask me at least two more times.*

Mercifully, Julie asked me what was wrong three times. I told her. Her answer was somewhat unmerciful.

"Well, you're not going to change that by hanging around here. You need to get yourself out there, Kara!"

I told her that was easy for her to say since she was apparently perfect and had a boyfriend, besides. This did not move the conversation forward.

"Fine," said Julie. "Don't take my advice." Then she went for a "quick run," which was pretty much her only option for avoiding me completely since I kinda promised my feet they'd never have to see the insides of my seventy-eight-dollar running shoes again.

I sighed a few more times, but to no avail. Mom and Dad are masters of ignoring pleas for attention. Which doesn't make sense, when you think about it. I mean, why have kids if you don't want to give attention to someone you gave life itself (and frizzy-haired, hazel-eyed genes)?

But even though I didn't like it, I did think about Julie's advice. Maybe I should get myself out there. And what better way to do that than to do what Anna and Tabbi suggested? Which is why I spent the rest of the morning creating my very own crafts blog!

While she's a master at ignoring pleas for attention, Mom didn't seem to mind helping me sign up for a Wordpress account at all. I came up with a cute name, took a bunch of pictures of the crafts I've already made, typed up directions, and uploaded them into a blog. It was easy! And fun! It's kinda great that now when I make something cool, I can show the world.

I need to post the URL for my new blog on Faceplace so the world, or at least my FP friends, can see that I am out there!

Here's my blog's home page:

The Gotta-Go Bag

Supplies Needed:
1. Depend Undergarment
2. Duct Tape
3. Scissors

Directions:
1. Place Depend on a flat surface
2. Tape up leg holes.
3. Select a cool color tape, then cover surface of Depend, leaving top open. (You might also leave a broad swath of the white Depend fabric uncovered for contrast. This will also make the statement "I am not ashamed!")
4. Once Depend is covered, add decorative duct tape details with contrasting colored tape.
5. Cut three four-foot-long pieces of duct tape and lay on a flat surface.
6. Fold each piece in half so sticky side of tape meets stick side. Now you have three duct tape strips.
7. Braid strips together to create a handle.
8. Secure handle to outside of Depend with more duct tape.
9. Add duct tape fringe if desired.

Voilà! You've just created the Gotta-Go-on-the-Go Bag. The only purse that can help you avoid life's little accidents!

About Me!

Hi! Welcome to my blog. I love creativity! — Kara

Things to Create!

- Gotta-Go-on-the-Go Bag
- Altoids Tin Suitcase
- Pedicured Pencil
- Bead & Button Doorway Curtain
- Wire Fish Pin

Sunday, February 25
Bedtime

Logged on to FP tonight and guess what—415 chicks and 238 dudes have taken my surveys. Awesome. And my results go right along with Bebe's tip this week. It still looks like confidence is a quality admired by both guys and girls.

To: Kara M <Craftychick@mailquickly.com>

From: BebeTruelove <bebe@bebetruelove.com>

Subject: Tip #7

Dear Soul Mate Seeker,

Your confidence will send the message that you're someone great to be with!

Tip #7: Be confident!

Good Luck in Love,

Bebe

TRY MIRROR-ME-GORGEOUS!
A PEEK INTO THIS MIRROR WITH GOLDEN OVERTONES WILL GIVE YOU THE CONFIDENCE YOU NEED BEFORE HEADING OUT! NEED A BOOST WHILE IN A CROWD? GET THE COMPACT-SIZED MINI-ME-GORGEOUS FREE WHEN YOU CLICK HERE TO ORDER NOW.
♥ MIRROR-ME ♥
(MUST BE 18 YEARS OF AGE TO ORDER.)

Oh, and my crafts blog already got a few hits, too. Hello, universe!

```
             WEEK 8: RESEARCH REVIEW
             # of subjects observed: 0
         (Officially, that I took notes on.
                 I'm getting slack.)

                     Findings:
      # of chicks who have taken FP survey: 415
         # of dudes who have taken it: 238

         Bebe Truelove's Tip #7: Be confident!
      (I'm thinking that this is easier for women with
                 luscious hair and lips.)

         Data Collection Methods: FP surveys
```

Monday, February 26
Third period

Today in English we had to write a descriptive paragraph about someone in the room. Then Mrs. Hill collected the papers and read the paragraphs aloud so we could guess who was being described.

The problem with the assignment was that Mrs. Hill didn't *tell* us ahead of time that our paragraphs would be read aloud. So even though she kept the authors anonymous, there was a lot of giggling and a few uncomfortable moments when our words were broadcast to the entire room. One of these uncomfortable moments occurred when Mrs. Hill read a paragraph that started like this:

"This person is pretty."

"Colleen!" yelled Maybelline.

"No interrupting!" snapped Mrs. Hill without smiling. But I think I detected a smile when she read the next sentence.

"Her hair has beautiful curls." (Everyone giggled except maybe Maybelline and The Sponge, because Maybelline's hair is ruler-straight.)

"She's very nice and she likes to read. She's funny and has a fantastic smile, especially when she laughs. She's also one of the most creative people I've ever known. She can make anything out of duct tape." (Now my face was burning.)

"Kara!" yelled practically everyone. Well, everyone but me and Maybelline. (I heard her mumble, "Kara's *not* pretty!")

I didn't care though. Because while it *is* embarrassing to hear stuff read about yourself, I have to admit it's also flattering. I canvassed the room and noticed Chip bending over, acting like he was tying his shoe. I could see that the back of his neck was Coca-Cola-logo red, so I know he's the one who wrote it. And I know that I don't mind that he was.

Tuesday, February 27
After my date. That's right. My date.

Horror of horrors and pinnacle of bad timing! After school, Julie barged into my room (I don't even bother locking the door anymore) and said, "Hey! Lyle and I are setting you up with Phillip. We'll double-date!"

"No," I said. "No way. I'm not going out with Lyle's brother."

"Got any better offers?"

"Not yet. But I might soon," I said, thinking of Chip. "Besides, if I *was* meant to be with Phil, I think I'd know that by now."

"You never know," said Julie, which kind of annoyed me because that's *my* catchphrase and it's really hard to find an argument against your own mantra. But I tried anyway.

"This is mortifying!" I yelled. "If Phillip wanted to ask me out, he'd have done it himself. It's like a sympathy date. And a sympathy date is worse than no date!"

"Look," she said. "We're going. It's the movies, not your wedding. Get over it."

"*You* look," I said. "I think I like someone else. If he finds out I went out with Phillip, it might make him back off."

"Fine," said Julie, tossing her ponytail. "Want out of the date? Call Phillip and break it." Julie won. She knew I'd never make that call.

And that is how I came to have my first real date ever and

to gather enough information about Phillip to realize that he's not and never will be my soul mate.

The guys picked us up in Lyle's used Volvo. I sat in the back with Phillip. He said, "Hi," and started looking out the window. Meanwhile, I was using all of my powers of concentration to will Chip to *not* be at the movies that night.

The film, which was supposed to be a comedy, was completely stupid. It was about four guys from this decade getting stuck fifty years in the past. The plot involved a lot of falling, getting stuck, and dressing like women to get out of awkward situations. It was the least romantic movie ever made, but that didn't keep Lyle and Julie from taking advantage of the darker moments to kiss!

Almost as soon as we got back in the car, Phillip got a text message. So he started texting someone while Julie carried on a fake-cheerful conversation about the movie. When we got to my house (Phillip still texting), I said thanks and ran inside because even if you're not really interested in a guy, and even if you truly find him boring, there's nothing worse than being ignored on a date.

Midnight

I can't sleep. Maybe it's because—in a way—things have gotten more exciting for me. I mean, I've had my first date.

(Even if it was a bummer.) I've had my first kiss. (Even if it was a bummer.) And I've even been written about! So despite the fact that I'm still just as boyfriendless as always, it seems like I'm getting closer to my goal. I decided to pull out my list again and see how the guys who gave me my first date, my first kiss, and my first descriptive paragraph rated.

I rewrote "The Perfect Soul Mate: A List (Revised)" as a list of questions so I'd have a clear picture of positive and negative responses.

Y answers improve rating.	Chip	Evan	Phillip
Is he nice?	Y	Y	Y
Is he funny?	Y	N	N
Does he read books?	Y	?	?
Does he like art? (duct tape counts)	Y	?	?
Does he think I'm great? (kisses count)	Y	Y	N
When asked if he teaches algebra, can he answer "no"?	Y	Y	Y
When asked if he has dated The Vine, can he answer "no"?	N	Y	Y
Does he have compassion?	Y	Y	N
Will he be there no matter what?	?	?	?

Just to get a clear visual of how these guys stack up (and because I still wasn't tired), I created a bar graph.

Three Possible Soul Mates

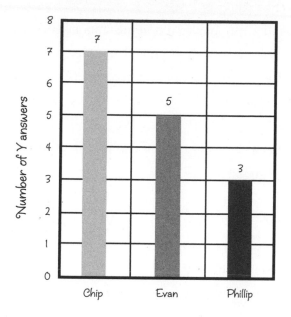

I ended up having to eliminate question number nine completely. Because how can I tell if any of these guys are going to "be there no matter what"? Most guys my age can't even tell you what their plans for the weekend are, never mind the rest of their lives. It seems like you'd have to know someone an awfully long time to be able to answer that question.

I guess I'd like to know that someday I'll find that "one person in the world who understands me completely and shares my hopes and dreams." Who wouldn't want that? And when I find him, I definitely want to be assured that he'll be there no matter what. That seems like a quality you'd just have to have in a soul mate.

So I looked at the bar graph again and asked myself two questions.

Q #1: After evaluating the data collected, can I tell who will be my soul mate?

A: No!

Q #2: After evaluating the data collected, can I tell who I would like to go out with?

A: Yes!

This led me to the following conclusion: I am too young to try to find my one and only soul mate! Does that mean I'm giving up this experiment?

No. Just going back to where I started.

THE SCIENTIFIC METHOD

Step 1: Ask a Question

How can I find a boyfriend?

Wednesday, February 28
Fourth period

Sooooooo . . . one evening with me, and Phillip Bernard asked someone else out. It makes me feel somewhat better to know that I'd already decided he wasn't a good candidate for the title of Kara's First Boyfriend. But still. It's like I drove him into her arms. Rumor has it that he and Anna Johnstone are now an item. I believe that rumor because Anna and Phillip were obviously holding hands under the table at lunch, even though Anna was looking down the whole time like she was embarrassed.

I like Anna. She's pretty but also very shy. As far as I know, she's only had one other boyfriend, Alex L, for a few days last year. It's easy not to notice her. But I guess Phillip did. It makes sense for two attractive, nice, and quiet (translation: boring) people to be together. Still, I can't help being embarrassed, because Anna and I have always been kind of *level two* friends. Not like me and Tabbi, but we do things together once in a while.

My brain is full of questions: Was it Anna who sent Phillip that post-movie text? Will her opinion of me change if she finds out about my "date" with her new boyfriend? Did Phillip ask out Anna the minute he finished his date with me? Maybe he even did it during the date. Maybe that's what the texting was about. Can anything be more humiliating than that?????!!!!

Part of me is happy that someone as nice as Anna found someone like Phillip to be with . . . but part of me wonders . . . *why can't I?????*

After school. Cloud nine.

My cell rang as soon as I flopped down on my fluffy white rug. It was Tabs. That girl has perfect timing. We had a wild conversation.

Tabs: I hope Evan will ask me to the spring dance.

Me: (*Gulp! Deep breath*) EVAN!!!???

Tabs: I just really believe that he's "the one." I know he's done some rotten things, but you're supposed to forgive people you truly love and I'm ready to forgive Evan.

Me: You're too good for him, Tabs.

Tabs: Just because he made some mistakes doesn't mean he's not a great person. I think he's sorry, I really do. That's why he tried to kiss you.

Me: Tabs —

Tabs: He had to know you'd tell me and he knew it'd make me jealous.

Me: Yeah. But you have a boyfriend. Evan won't ask you to the dance as long as you're dating James.

Tabs: Evan had a girlfriend when Maybelline asked him to the dance and he said yes.

Me: Point taken. But why not make yourself more available by breaking up with James?

Tabs: *Because* (Tabbi sounded exasperated), I don't want to be *alone*.

I got off of the phone ASAP after that comment! Being alone isn't that bad!

P.S. Okay, I guess having a boyfriend you really like is better than being alone. Then again, how would *I* know?

Thursday, March 1
Lunch

I can't believe that a real live person of the opposite sex has finally asked me out (without being forced) and it's someone who's totally off-limits. Evan just now caught up with me as I was entering the cafeteria and asked me to the spring dance. This falls into the "Be careful what you wish for: It might come true" category. I'm hoping, for Tabbi's sake, that she doesn't find out because she'll talk herself into thinking it's another sign that he wants her back, which I know for a fact is absolutely not the case. Here's what he said when I suggested he ask Tabbi instead:

"I've already caught that fish."

(!)

Isn't that a totally rude thing for him to say about a person whose name he used to wear on his hand?

Then he said, "You're more interesting than Tabbi."

"So why didn't you just ask me out in the first place?" The question just popped out of my mouth.

"You were too quiet back then."

I have to admit that when I used to drag Tabbi with me to seek out Evan, I let her do most of the talking. I was afraid I'd say something stupid. Once he was off-limits, I didn't really care what I said. I guess there is some small comfort knowing that he likes me better now that I'm acting more like myself. Not that it matters as far as Evan is concerned. It's okay, though. I wouldn't want to end up being just another fish to him anyway.

Here come Tabbi and James. Time to close this journal and open my lunch!

After school

I expected things to change after Mrs. Hill read that descriptive paragraph that Chip wrote about me. I mean, if he said all that nice stuff (and I *know* he did), then that must mean he likes me, right? Plus, it wasn't that long ago that I overheard him tell Jonah Nate that I was out of Jonah Nate's league. That's good, right? He even kind of broke up with The Vine because of me, right?

But Chip talks to me less now than ever. He never sits near me during lunch anymore and it's been weeks since he's come up with any new funny fake names to share.

Today I decided I might as well try being proactive again. After all, Bebe's tip for the week is "be confident." So I sat right down behind him before Mrs. Hill's class started. He said "Hi, Kara" friendly enough, but then he got up to go sharpen his pencil and left me sitting there. (!) It was way awkward. My confidence zoomed back to my assigned seat and I followed it.

Talk about frustrating. I finally think I have a chance to do some real research (of the holding-hands-and-kissing variety) on someone who *actually likes me*, and now this.

It's pointless to ask Tabs for advice because she'll just tell me to raise my standards. Plus, she didn't exactly ask for my opinion before she started dating James! (And yes, I would have told her to raise her standards.)

Still, feeling the need to talk to *someone*, I finally turned to Julie. At least it *looks* like she's been successful in the boyfriend search. I told her the story, starting with the descriptive paragraph.

"Chip *obviously* likes you," said Julie, "but *surely* you realize he's mortified that his feelings were read aloud."

"Well, it seems like he'd at least *talk to me*, then."

"Sometimes when people start crushing on each other, it's actually harder to talk than before," Julie explained. I think she's right about that. I remember how I ran out of A&F that time.

"But why don't I have issues talking to *Chip*, since I think I have a crush on him, too?"

Julie heaved a big ol' sigh to show what she thought of my question. I hate when she does that. "Because you already *know* your crush likes you back. Meanwhile, he's putting himself out there to be crushed by his crush."

"So how do I let him know I like him?"

"Tell him."

"Julie! I can't do that!"

"Well," said Julie. "Be Extreme Kara."

"Huh?"

"Figure out what attracted Chip to you in the first place and emphasize those qualities. That's how I got Lyle to notice me."

"Really?"

"Yep. Lyle's athletic and into biking, so I thought I'd have a better chance with him if he knew I was athletic, too."

Hey! I knew she was trying to get Lyle to notice her when we took those many laps down Hobby Lane, but I didn't realize she was trying to get him to notice a *particular quality* about her: her athleticism. If it worked for Julie, I may as well try it. If only I could figure out which of my many good qualities to take to the extreme level. HA!

Friday, March 2
Before school

Evan wasted no time in casting his net again. He's already asked Monique Bishop to the spring dance. A sixth grader!

Poor Tabbi. Her eyes are that post-crying watery-red color. Yet she said it doesn't bother her "one bit." In fact, she's said "I don't care" so many times this morning that it's obvious she does care. When someone says "I don't care" once, you can pretty much take it at face value. But if you multiply that by ten or twenty, it's like the double-negative thing. Which is why I'm positive that Tabbi is crushed.

Lunch

It was the best lunch period EVER! That's because two brand-new subjects walked into the cafeteria and both were more delicious-looking than anything that's ever been served in the place. Apparently, Jake and Josh Baxter *just* enrolled in my school.

When they walked through the doors, all conversation stopped, then turned to the cute new twins. (And to whom the cute new twins will take to the dance.) Unfortunately, it's hard to get close enough to them to make a really decent observation with all of the queen bees swarming around.

The Vine is working hard to put down roots next to one of them, and The Sponge is stuck to them like a stamp to an envelope. You can just see those tiny wheels in her head turning. She must be *dying* to get Josh and Jake to take her on the double date of her dreams. In her world, what could be more perfect than a date who's absolutely identical to Maybelline's? I doubt that Maybelline is interested, since she has an older man, but you never know. Those Baxter twins sure are cute.

Subjects #15 and #16: JAKE AND JOSH BAXTER
Data Collected on: 3/2   Status: Single (But it's only a
Hair: Strawberry blond   matter of time . . .)
Eyes: Sky blue
Eyebrows: Pale, but nicely arched
Body Type: Tall and toasty
Age: 13
Nice-o-meter: ☺☺☺☺☺
Interest Level: ♥♥♥♥♥ (Who wouldn't be interested?)

Saturday, March 3
Bedtime

Fourteen days. That's how long we have until the dance. It seems like the *perfect* opportunity for Chip to ask me out, if he really does like me. But apparently Chip is not an opportunity seizer. And being "Extreme Kara" isn't working.

I've been over the qualities about me that Chip seemed to like (according to his descriptive paragraph) and I've tried to emphasize the ones that I could. They are:

1. Pretty (If he really thinks that, he's the only one.)
2. Beautiful curls (I've abandoned my hair dryer and have been wearing my hair loose!)
3. Nice (That comes naturally. Ha.)
4. Likes to read (Just to show how much I like to read, I've been lugging around *Princess Academy*, which is a book about a girl who has a chance to fall in love with a prince but discovers that she loves someone she grew up with. *Sigh.*)
5. Funny (This one's hard to force. I mean I can't exactly walk up to someone who hasn't spoken to me in days and say, "Knock knock . . .")
6. Fantastic smile (I've been grinning till my teeth hurt.)
7. Creative — can make anything out of duct tape (I made a new belt to go with my bag, but Chip hasn't seemed to notice. What am I supposed to do . . . cover myself in duct tape?)

I'm starting to feel defeated. Maybe it wasn't even Chip who wrote that paragraph. Maybe, for some reason, I'd just hoped it was.

Sunday, March 4
Morning

I was in no mood to read Bebe's latest e-mail when I woke up today, but it ended up putting me in a good mood.

To: Kara M <Craftychick@mailquickly.com>
From: BebeTruelove <bebe@bebetruelove.com>
Subject: Tip #9

Dear Soul Mate Seeker,
A guy likes a girl who shows she's one of a kind. Do you like big bags? Silky scarves? Bright lipstick? Don't be afraid to show the world who you are!

Tip #9: Show your style!

Good Luck in Love,
Bebe

See why this gives me hope? If carrying a bag made from a giant diaper and duct tape isn't style, I don't know what is!

Afternoon

Question: If Chip actually likes me, and I kinda like him back, that's pretty close to having a boyfriend, isn't it?

It was a quiet afternoon, so I had a lot of time to ponder this question. It seemed that I'd traveled to the brink of boyfriendhood but that was as far, apparently, as I was going to get. Let me tell you, the brink of what is sure to be an awesome experience is not an ideal destination. Especially when you've dedicated your life, or at least the last two months, to the science of researching boys.

There must be something that I'm missing. I sat down at my dresser and took a good long look in the mirror at the girl who, according to that descriptive paragraph Mrs. Hill read, is pretty and has a fantastic smile and beautiful curls.

Truthfully, I don't think I look that bad. Sure, any time I look in the mirror I see *some* things I don't like. Most days,

I wish I had Julie's hair, or that I didn't have a zit on my cheek or something.

But I'm wondering about that part of myself that I can't see in the mirror. That part that Bebe Truelove calls the soul. See, I've always kind of assumed that part of me was great, and that if I could get everyone to see how great that part is, I'd have a boyfriend for sure. But what if my invisible self isn't so perfect? What if there is something about me that needs to change before I get into a relationship?

While I was thinking about this, I realized I had the perfect source of information under my very own roof: Julie! Ms. Sabatino would call her a "primary source."

Even though I've talked to my sister about boys before, I've never done it officially. You know—as a scientist. So I decided to conduct an interview with her for my Hidden Agenda Boyfriend Research Project.

I grabbed a pen and notebook and went to her room, and, unlike her, stood in the hall and waited instead of barging in.

Julie answered the door with her cell phone clamped between her shoulder and her chin. She was talking to someone else on the phone, but her eyes talked to me. They said *go away*. I wasn't about to let a cell phone conversation stand in the way of scientific research, however. Luckily, I knew just what to say to get her to agree to answer my questions. Here is a transcript of the interview.

JULIE McALLISTER INTERVIEW

Date: Sunday, March 4
Time: 3:37 p.m.
Location: Julie's Room
Persons Present: Kara McAllister (Interviewer)
    Julie McAllister (Respondent)

Interviewer: Can I interview you for a research project?
Respondent: No.
Interviewer: I'll tell Mom you made me stop running with you so you could be with Lyle.
Respondent *(Into the phone that was still in chin-shoulder clutch)*: Call you back in a minute, okay? *(To interviewer. Eyes still saying* go away *but mouth now participating in interview.)* Fine. First question?
Interviewer: How old are you?
Respondent: Kara! Stop wasting time!
Interviewer: Just being professional. Second question. Approximately how many boyfriends have you had?
Respondent: *(Says nothing. Shrugs. Shrugs!!! Which is universal language for these two phrases:* too many to count *AND* I'm too important to be bothered with such trivial details! *That shrug is proof of something I've been suspecting for a long time. My sister is officially one of the luckiest people on Earth.)*

Questions the World's Luckiest People Can Answer with a Shrug:

1. How many boyfriends have you had?
2. How much gold is in the vault, Your Majesty?
3. Does your extensive art collection happen to include a Picasso?
4. Was Robert Pattinson able to attend the all-celebrity party you hosted on your yacht?

Respondent: Well?

Interviewer: Well what? *(Zoning back in after the shrug.)*

Respondent: Please tell me this interview is over. *(Note: When respondent said "interview," she used air quotes. Grrrrrr.)*

Interviewer: No. In your experience, what is the best way to get a guy to notice you?

Respondent: *(Shrugs)*

Interviewer: Aaack! Stop with the shrugging! Answer me!

Respondent: I don't know. I haven't really thought about it.

Interviewer: Think about it.

Respondent: Hmmm. I guess the first step is to find a way to be alone with your crush.

Interviewer: (*Scribbling notes*) Why is that important?

Respondent: Because guys act differently when they're around other people. They might be afraid to give you attention if they think their buds are watching.

Interviewer: Hey! Wait a minute! That's why you outran me when we went jogging. You wanted to be alone with Lyle.

Respondent: (*Laughs*) I did. And I'd do it again. Any more questions?

Interviewer: Not right now. Thanks, Julie!

END TRANSCRIPT

I couldn't keep interviewing Julie after that because I was too excited. See, I think she was onto something. Something that might be the key to the whole reason I can't seem to get a boyfriend.

Look at how Tabbi got Evan. She sat with him when I wasn't there and she was *alone*. And look how Chicken Girl got Justin. She pulled him into a dressing room so she could be *alone* with him. And The Vine . . . she's found a way to be *alone* with a guy in a room full of people just by cuddling up to him and sitting too close for anyone to get between them.

As further evidence, I offer up the one time I have ever been kissed. I was *alone* (unfortunately, in the boys' bathroom) with Evan. So maybe I just need to find a way to be *alone* with Chip! Only not in the boys' bathroom.

```
            WEEK 9: RESEARCH REVIEW
            # of subjects observed: 2

                     Findings:
      # of chicks who have taken FP survey: 834
         # of dudes who have taken it: 517
          Woo-hoo! This survey rocks.


       Bebe Truelove's Tip #9: Show your style!


              Data Collection Methods:
           interview, observations, survey
```

Monday, March 5
First period

I had the perfect opportunity to be *alone* with Chip today! When I walked into the lunchroom, he was at a table by himself. So I walked right over there and sat down with him! But he didn't ask me to the dance like I thought he might once we were *alone*. Still, what he did ask wasn't all that bad.

He wants me to make four duct tape wallets for him to give as gifts. When I asked him what colors, he said, "I'll leave it up to you. Everything you do turns out really cool." Then, suddenly, I couldn't think of anything to say.

Lunch

My predictions were true. The Sponge did have her eye on one of the twins. She actually asked Jake to the spring dance. Jake is the one with a *slightly* thinner face and *slightly* longer hair and he's *slightly* less cute than Josh. (But he's still as hot as Tabasco, believe me.) It's like The Sponge knew that if she wanted to date one of the twins while Maybelline dated the other, she'd have to take Jake because Maybelline would, of course, get the cuter one.

But get this: Jake said he was bringing his girlfriend from his old school to the dance. Then Josh, who was standing right there, said he'd be glad to go with The Sponge. You could almost hear The Sponge's brain whirring, trying to figure out if she should take the cuter one or leave him for Maybelline. In then end she came to her senses. She said "Great!" and walked away giggling.

After school

It's like *everyone* else is connected by some invisible network on Planet Boyfriend and I'm out in space. A moon connected to no one. Orbiting alone.

I mean, how can someone with no personality get two decent dates and I can't even get one? (Evan no longer qualifies as decent.) I ask this because while we were sitting in science waiting for the bell, Alex Langford knelt down beside Tiffany's desk and said, "Don't go to the dance with that twin. Go with me." (!)

Then The Sponge said, "Oh, Alex." She got tears in her eyes, and she and Alex started hugging right behind Ms. Sabatino's back. But it wasn't the kinda hug that says *Gee, it's great to see you, Uncle Mel.* The hug between The Sponge and Alex said something more like *Don't get on that plane! Don't do it! I can't live without you!* Then Ms. Sabatino turned around and they were suddenly hugging right in front of her face. Ms. S is cool and all, but she still wrote them up and sent them to the office, referral slips in hands.

Yet Alex L and Tiffany didn't look like two kids in trouble when they walked out of the room. They looked really happy. In fact, I've never seen happier faces on kids holding referral slips. And I have to wonder, if The Sponge really cared for Alex (and she had to after that mega hug), why didn't she tell him a long time ago? Did she really break up with someone she liked just to be like Maybelline?

Oh well, no matter what the answers are, I think there might be more to The Sponge than I thought.

Tuesday, March 6
On the bus

I just gave Chip his wallets. I felt funny making him pay for them, so I tried to give him a two-for-one deal, but he wouldn't take it. Which isn't all bad—*cha-ching*—sixty bucks! I made two red ones, a green one, and a pink and black one (just to see what he'd say). I made about ten of them before I got four that I thought were perfect. It's okay though. I uploaded pictures of the other six to my new blog. I've gotten great comments!

Anyway, Chip opened all of the wallets and turned them over carefully in his hands. He really got into examining them and he asked a lot of questions about how they were constructed. He laughed when he saw the pink and black one. He said he knew just who to give that one to. He thought it was cool. He thought they were all cool. The boy seems to like anything made out of duct tape.

Homework time

That's it! I *will* cover myself with duct tape to get Chip to notice me. Not literally, of course. Well, almost literally. I had the idea when I was thinking about how to dress for the dance. I tried to get Mom to take me to the mall to get me a new outfit, but she refused. She said, "Last time you begged for something new from the mall, you only wore them ten times before pushing them to the back of your closet. Don't think I didn't notice."

She was talking about the running shoes. Okay, I admit it. I *did* think she hadn't noticed. I got tired of wearing them to school every day trying to wear them out, and Julie never came up with a better plan that allowed us to stop running together, *like she was supposed to*, so I just tried to make the shoes disappear.

This meant I was stuck with no date AND no cute dress to sport! Until I came up with a great idea . . .

I remembered seeing those prom dresses made out of duct tape when I was researching bag styles! So I figured if you can make a prom dress from duct tape, why not a party dress? I did a little more online research and found that you can make duct tape clothes in four easy steps:

1. Cover big sheets of paper with duct tape.
2. Lay pieces of selected pattern on top of duct tape sheets.

3. Cut out pattern.
4. Following pattern directions, tape pieces together instead of sewing.

I went back to Mom and asked her if she could take me to the hardware store instead of the mall. Then I told her my plan. She LOVED it.

Mom always goes for us experimenting with creative expression. Really, the woman's never met a craft she didn't like. She even helped me search online for a pattern. (We chose a simple sleeveless dress from *Teen Vogue*.) Tomorrow we shop for duct tape!

Friday, March 9
After dinner

Mom and I've been working on the duct tape dress for two days. I bought three rolls of black tape, one pink, and one green. My idea was to make the dress all black but to add some pink and green flowers to the shoulders. It is spring, after all.

We'd almost finished the dress when Julie decided to barge into the room with Lyle and Phillip in tow. Apparently, Lyle is Phillip's ride to baseball practice. The good news is that they went nuts over the dress. They thought it was the coolest, especially the zigzag pattern I'd cut along the hemline.

The bad news is that now someone at my school knows. And I wanted it to be a surprise. I told Phillip NOT to tell anyone about it. He said, "Who'd I tell?"

I resisted the urge to mention Anna, who I know would tell Tabbi, who would then know I was up to something. BUT I tried to play it cool, so I just shrugged. (I used the *I can't be bothered with such trivial details* variety.)

I have to confess that Phillip's and Lyle's reactions made me feel pretty good about my latest creation. I think the dress will "show my style" in a big way! (I hope Bebe's right about that last tip.) I'm a little worried, though, because my mimi always says, "There's a fine line between an outfit and a costume." And in the back of my mind, I've been wondering: Does duct tape clothing cross that line?

Sunday, March 11
Is 4:45 afternoon or evening? 'Cause that's what time it is.

It seems like Bebe is giving me a little nudge in the direction of a certain Chip Tyler. Right in time for the dance, too.

To: Kara M <Craftychick@mailquickly.com>

From: BebeTruelove <bebe@bebetruelove.com>

Subject: Tip #10

Dear Soul Mate Seeker,

Afraid of rejection? Don't be. Everyone faces it from time to time. But the more times you try, the greater your chances of success. Don't let fear keep you from approaching a possible soul mate.

Tip #10: Banish fear!

Good Luck in Love,

Bebe

TRY FEAR-CATCHERS!
MODELED AFTER NATIVE AMERICAN DREAM CATCHERS, THESE FEAR-
CATCHERS WILL HANG FROM YOUR KEY RING AND KEEP FEAR AT BAY.
AN ANCIENT SPELL IS SPOKEN OVER EACH FEAR-CATCHER
BEFORE IT LEAVES THE FACTORY!
CLICK HERE TO ORDER NOW!
♥ FEAR-CATCHERS ♥
(MUST BE 18 YEARS OF AGE TO ORDER.)

```
                  WEEK 10: RESEARCH REVIEW
                         Findings:
        # of chicks who have taken FP survey: 1,367
             # of dudes who have taken it: 821

     I'm presenting next week! I'll have tons of data!

         Bebe Truelove's Tip #10: Banish fear!

           Data Collection Method: surveys
```

Monday, March 12
Lunch

Chip asked me if I am going to the dance!

Okay, it isn't as good as if he'd actually asked me *to* the dance. But it does mean he cares whether I go or not. Doesn't it?

After dinner

At least there is still hope that maybe there's a boyfriend for me somewhere out there even if things don't work out with Chip. Because today I discovered an important fact that will help me with my research: There are quiet, inconspicuous guys just waiting to be noticed. I found this out after school because Anna, Tabs, and I ended up being partners for Mrs. Hill's "magazine project."

Luckily, Anna invited us over to her house to work on it. I quickly accepted. (I did NOT want to have them do it at my house, in case Lyle and Julie were there. If Lyle said something about my "date" with Phillip, I'd die.)

Anyway . . . we got to Anna's and it turns out she has an older brother named Paul. I asked her why she hadn't told us her brother was so cute. She said, "You wouldn't think about him that way if you ever saw him play those online battle games with his friends. Total geek fleet."

But Paul was really nice. Quiet, like Anna. He has a cleft chin that makes him look movie-star-ish. And he's in ninth grade, which means he was at my school last year and I never noticed him. This made me wonder if there are a lot of other quiet, cute guys out there that I haven't even considered yet.

When I got home, Mom asked me how the project was going. Since Anna, Tabs, and I ended up chatting the whole time instead of actually working on it, I tried to distract Mom—for some reason—by bringing up Anna's cute but geeky older brother.

Mom's comment was: "Don't count out the geeks! They usually have better earning potential than your run-of-the-mill jock." She smiled. "Dad was a geek and look at him now."

I looked. Yeah. I think this is the last time I'll be writing about Paul.

Subject Number #17: PAUL JOHNSTONE

Data Collected on: 3/12   Status: Single

Hair: Sandy blond, straight   (Anna is betting forever.)

Eyes: Greenish brown

Eyebrows: Nice

Body Type: Skinny in a way that suggests he'll always be nerdy.

Age: 15

Nice-o-meter: ☺☺☺☺☺

Interest Level: ♥♥♥

Thursday, March 15
Sixth period

Okay, it's too bad that my redo science fair project was due after the actual science fair because it totally would have beaten The Sponge's lame-but-first-place project involving strawberry smoothies! Oh well. The important thing is that Ms. Sabatino loved my new science project! She erased the F+ from the grade book and replaced it with a B. Which, of course, isn't as good as the A I might have made if not for Mr. DeLacey, but still. Here's what I presented to the class:

Male and female teens are looking for different things in relationships.

Materials

Computer with Internet access

Experiment

Distribute survey regarding relationships to teens on Facebook.

❈ Relationships: Do Girls and Guys Want the Same Things? ❈

Results:

Question 1: While 75% of guys felt it important that a girl have similar or the same interests, only 50% of girls felt this way.

Question 2: Girls found looks less important than guys. 88% of males surveyed felt that girls needed to at least look good to get their attention, compared to 57% of females.

Question 3: 95% of guys like it when a girl shows she's interested. Girls, on the other hand, are more willing to take risks.

Question 4: Girls (86%) find it important for guys to show confidence! Fewer guys, on the other hand, felt that confidence was important, though the majority (75%) found that it was.

Question 5: Teen girls are more interested in long-term relationships than teen boys. 17% are looking for their soul mate as opposed to only 2% of guys.

❈ Procedures ❈

1. Create survey asking questions in five key areas of interest regarding relationships for teens.
2. Introduce surveys to Facebook friends.
3. Allow time for surveys to be passed around the Internet.
4. Compile answers to surveys.
5. Compare results of surveys.

❈ Conclusion

Research supports hypothesis. Boys and girls are looking for different things in relationships, especially long-term relationships.

237

I felt pretty good about it, even though right in the middle of my presentation Maybelline sneered, "That survey is bogus. What does Kara know about love?"

"A lot more than I used to," I said. I wished I hadn't. Everyone started making those "wooooooooo" singsongy sounds that aren't actually words but can be translated as *I've just found out some great big secret about you.*

"That's not what I mean!" I said, blushing. "But if you look at the data collected from 2,188 teens, you'll see that even though guys and girls are attracted to each other, they are basically looking for different things in relationships."

The room got pretty quiet while I explained the results. (Told you, Mrs. Willis, that we were more interested in relationships than the Civil War!)

The most important thing I learned is that most guys aren't even looking for a soul mate yet. And that seventy-five percent of guys really do like girls with confidence! I need to work on that.

After class, a lot of people stood around asking questions, like I'm suddenly some kind of authority on love. Move over, Bebe Truelove!

Friday, March 16
After school

Well, my science fair project is finally over! The research is done. The hypothesis is supported. The results are published. That's one research project down and one to go.

It is time to compile my data and attempt to come up with a hypothesis for my more important Hidden Agenda Boyfriend Project. Here is a review of some of the most significant data I collected:

1. Unobtrusive Observations: Boy Subjects

After observing a variety of subjects, I've deduced that Subject #5 is interested in me.

2. Unobtrusive Observations: Girl Subjects

I observed the methods used by three girls when approaching their crushes. They all did it differently, but they had two things in common.

- Each girl had the confidence to approach her crush even if she *had* to realize (Gina the Vine) that some approaches would end in rejection.
- Each girl was successful at least some of the time.

3. Interview (Primary Source)

The interview I conducted revealed that it is important for a girl to approach her crush when he is alone.

4. Expert Advice (Primary Source)

Bebe Truelove says that a girl should show her style and

her confidence. (She says a lot of other stuff, too!)

5. Faceplace Surveys

The data collected from the surveys supports Bebe's advice about confidence. It also supports my earlier conclusion that I'm too young to be looking for a soul mate.

So. I've found a guy who is interested in me. And I've found an awesome way to show my style!

I think I've also found that invisible part of me that needs improving: The fact is, I'm a big chicken! Like I've said before, I like myself just fine. I do! But I'm not confident that boys are going to like me. *I'm afraid of rejection.*

But after analyzing the data, I think if I can find the courage to face possible rejection, my hypothesis will be supported.

THE SCIENTIFIC METHOD

Step 3: Form a Hypothesis

If I am confident and show interest (and my style) in the boy who has expressed interest in me, then I will have a boyfriend by the end of the dance tomorrow.

Saturday, March 17
After the dance

At first I thought my custom-designed duct tape dress plan had backfired on me in a big way. Tabbi promised she'd be at the dance when I arrived so I wouldn't be alone, but when I walked through the gym doors, my BFF was nowhere. Well, I guess she was somewhere, but since she wasn't where I needed her to be, she may as well have been nowhere. Here's who was there: Maybelline.

She took one look at my dress and burst out laughing. "What'd you do, Kara, make your own dress? Puh-lease tell me you're posting directions on your blog, because I'm gonna need them if I ever want to make something that hideous." When she said the word "blog," she used air quotes. I hate air quotes!

Despite the fact that I rode all the way to the dance reminding myself that seventy-five percent of guys like girls who are self-confident, this scientific knowledge evaporated under the heat of Maybelline's burning comments. I couldn't think of anything to say. So when she turned to laugh with The Sponge, I backed into the shadows, where no one would notice me. No one did. When I thought about how successful I was at going unnoticed, it was pretty depressing. . . .

Eventually, Tabs entered with James. She took, like, fifteen seconds to glance around before hitting the dance floor. Thanks, BFF!

A little later, Chip came in alone. He was dressed like the other guys, but I thought he looked particularly nice in his khaki pants, button-down shirt, and tie. I watched him walk over to the refreshment table and get a soda. Then he stood across the room and looked around. I held my breath, hoping he would notice me and then run toward me, arms outstretched, asking me to dance. Then I would know for sure that he liked me. But I am never that lucky. When Chip's eyes reached me in the shadows they slid right over me. Was I just successfully blending in, or had he seen me and decided that he'd rather not notice a girl in a homemade duct tape dress?

One thing was for sure. If I stayed in the shadows all night, I'd never know. It was time for:

```
                 THE SCIENTIFIC METHOD

     Step 4: Experiment. Test Your Hypothesis.

  Procedure used to confirm or disprove hypothesis:

     Girl banishes fear, shows her style, displays
        confidence, and walks toward her crush.
```

"Wow." That's what Chip said when I got close enough for him to really see my *Teen Vogue* duct tape dress with roses on the strap. He reached out and touched the roses, and when he did, his hand brushed my shoulder and it gave me that tingly feeling!

"That dress is amazing."

"Thanks," I said. I could feel my face heating up, but it wasn't the Mouth of Hades chili type of hot. More like the snuggled-under-a-blanket-drinking-cocoa kind of hot.

"Kara, you can do anything." Chip smiled.

"No I can't," I said, but I smiled back.

"Well, can you dance?" he asked.

I nodded and we headed to the dance floor, which was really the gym floor. But the gym was decorated with lots of balloons, glittery golden streamers, and colorful lights, so it really didn't seem like an athletic facility. We danced for, like, five songs in a row. It was great! But let me just say that if you go to a dance in a dress made of strips of plastic, be sure to create a short hemline and make it sleeveless, like I did. Man, did I sweat! So I didn't really mind when Tabs pulled me aside to "freshen up" even though what she actually intended to do was accost me in the girls' room.

Tabbi waved her finger at me and said, "Kara, you look like you're really enjoying dancing with Chip! Please tell me it's an act. *Please* do not say that you have a crush on that goof."

"I'm just doing research, but you're right. I'm enjoying it," I said. "Remember, James was pretty goofy, too, at the beginning of the year."

Tabbi changed the subject. "Why didn't you *tell* me you were making something cool to wear? I could have made one too!" Which might have been a *teeny tiny* part of the reason I didn't tell her, now that I think about it. But I was glad she liked it.

Tabs and James danced near us for the rest of the night. The tiny, swirling lights bouncing off the disco ball made it seem like we were being sprinkled with fairy dust as they passed over our skin and dressy clothes. Everyone looked better that night than they do at school, and everyone looked happier! It was überfuntastic! And I was glad I had a chance to see Tabs pretend to gag when Evan boogied by, clinging to Monique. I think she's finally over him!

When the dance was almost over Chip offered to walk me home, so I called Mom. She said it'd be okay as long as I got to the house in fifteen minutes. She also mentioned that she'd be looking out the window, watching for me to come down the street. That's a bit overprotective, don't you think?

I gave her message to Chip and he gave a little frown before flipping open his cell to check the time. "Well, we'd better get going."

As soon as we got outside, Chip held out his hand and I took it. His palm was warm and he squeezed my fingers.

I'd never held hands with a boy before—well, not in that way—and it felt really, really good.

We were about five houses from mine when Chip stopped to check his phone again. "We have five whole minutes."

He took my other hand and pulled me closer. I pulled back.

"What?" he said.

"I don't know . . . it's just . . . I'm not sure I can like a guy who let Gina Johns crawl all over him." (It still bothered me. I couldn't push it out of my mind.)

"Come on, Kara," he said, putting his arms around my waist. "You should thank her. 'Cause if it weren't for her, I wouldn't know how to do this."

Then he touched my face, leaned down, and kissed me. Which feels a whole lot better than holding hands.

When I opened my eyes, Chip was smiling at me. Talk about a fantastic smile! I smiled back . . . until I saw our front porch light blink on like a warning beacon.

"I need to go," I said.

Chip nodded and slid his hand into mine again. Then, holding hands, we walked to the door.

Subject Number #5: CHIP TYLER (Card 3)
Data Collected on: 3/17   Status: Taken!!
Hair: Cute
Eyes: Windows to a great-looking soul
Eyebrows: Nice
Body Type: Good
Age: 13
Nice-o-meter: ☺☺☺☺☺
Interest Level: ♥♥♥♥♥♥♥♥♥♥♥♥♥♥♥♥♥♥♥♥♥♥♥♥♥♥♥♥♥♥♥♥♥

Sunday, March 18
Early. Too early. But I'm too excited to sleep. Too too excited.

I have asked a question. I have researched. I have formed a hypothesis. I have performed an experiment. I am now ready for:

```
           THE SCIENTIFIC METHOD
         Step 5: Interpret Your Data
    Subject #5 reacted positively to researcher
      when she performed the experiment cited
                  in Step 4.

                   Evidence:
   1. Said "Wow" when he saw researcher showing
            her style in duct tape dress.
   2. Asked researcher to dance when she stepped
                out of the shadows.
   3. Held researcher's hand and kissed her after
       she had the confidence to approach him.
```

After analyzing the data above and adding it to the fact that Chip has sent me fourteen texts since the dance, one of which asked if I could go to the movies tonight, I have a pretty good idea of what my conclusion is going to be. (I have *got* to figure out another way to get Mom and Dad to spring for unlimited texting since my plan for making an A in science didn't work out! Maybe it's time to sell more duct tape creations. . . .)

```
THE SCIENTIFIC METHOD

Step 6: Draw a Conclusion

Conclusion: Research Supports Hypothesis

If you banish fear, show your style, and show
   confidence when approaching a boy who is
interested in you, you might end up with a
             boyfriend. Like I did!
```

After lunch at the McAllister Café, where the food is free but not exciting

This afternoon I got another message from Bebe Truelove, along with an ad for a *Romantic Atlantic Singles Cruise.*

To: Kara M <Craftychick@mailquickly.com>
From: BebeTruelove <bebe@bebetruelove.com>
Subject: You can keep receiving Bebe's great advice!

Dear Soul Mate Seeker,

Have you found your soul mate yet? If so, let me know!
I'll add your name to the growing list of souls who have

found mates by following my advice. That list is currently over 950 names strong! If you haven't, don't give up hope! You can continue getting advice from me, Bebe Truelove, once a week for the next year for only $19.95. Just go to the *subscribe* page at my web address and enter your credit card number. You must be 18 years or older to subscribe.

Yours in Luck and Love,

Bebe

TAKE A SINGLES CRUISE!
WHAT BETTER PLACE TO MEET YOUR SOUL MATE THAN ON THE
ROMANTIC ATLANTIC? DON'T MISS THE VOYAGE OF A LIFETIME!
CLICK HERE TO BOOK YOUR TRIP!
♥ ROMANTIC ATLANTIC ♥
(MUST BE 18 YEARS OF AGE TO ORDER.)

I'm starting to feel like Bebe might be a scam artist. I guess there's a chance that her advice helps some people find soul mates. But maybe it's just that covering yourself with Love-Mist body spray while wearing a red velvet bikini on a singles cruise brings luck in love.

Besides, I found that some of her tips could be improved by changing just a few little words. Take Tip #1: Be yourself. This is not the greatest advice. But if you add just two words, it fixes everything. If I were sending out advice, my first tip would be: Be *true* to yourself.

In other words, it's important to stick to your values. But

maybe there are things about yourself that you can improve without changing your values. Things that might change your life! Or at least your social life . . . ☺

Anyway, I am not going to sign up to keep getting advice from Bebe. Why would I? I'm no longer looking for love!

Have to go. My parents are actually letting me go out on my first real date tonight! By *real*, I mean a date where the boy isn't forced by his older brother to go out with me. Chip and I are double-dating with Tabs and James. . . .

Past bedtime (According to my parents). But I am too excited to sleep. Again.

Going to the movies with someone who actually likes me is a whole new experience, let me tell you. After the movie, we went out for pizza. It was a blast! I think Tabbi is warming up to Chip, and James isn't so bad.

The guys want to go out again on Wednesday. Right. The only way my parents will let that happen is if I finish Mrs. Hill's magazine project before then, and that's pretty unlikely. Tabs, Anna, and I have tons of work to do, since we basically goofed off the whole time at Anna's house. Homework doesn't go away, even when you finally get a boyfriend.

BTW, I finally got up the nerve to ask Chip why he didn't

kiss me that time we played spin the bottle. His answer surprised me. He said he was scared I wouldn't kiss him back! I totally would have, since I was so curious about kissing. But it wouldn't have been as good because I didn't feel the same way about him back then.

While I'm on the subject of kissing, let me just say that kissing a boy who might be your soul mate (you never know) beneath the stars on a cool spring night is a whole lot better than kissing a boy who's your best friend's ex beneath a ringing bell in a stinky restroom. Pretty much every kiss I've shared with Chip (all three of them) is so much better than the one I had with Evan that it's like comparing a piece of chocolate cake with fudge icing to asparagus soup. I don't know . . . kissing him just feels right.

All in all, I'd say my Hidden Agenda Boyfriend Research Project has been a huge success. It is time for the final step of the scientific method!

```
            THE SCIENTIFIC METHOD

            Step 7: Publish Results

      Done! Here it is! You're reading it!
```

Ahhhhhh. It feels great to be done with the project!

Wait. I'm just checking over my notes here. Aaarrrrgh! There's one more step to the scientific method.

```
THE SCIENTIFIC METHOD

Step 8: Retest
```

Retest? Are you KIDDING me? I've spent months compiling this very private data. I am NOT going through that again. Especially since I'm busier than ever. Now that I have a boyfriend, I don't expect to have every single weekend free, for one thing.

Also, I can tell that my blog is going to take a lot of time. It's worth it, though. I posted pictures of my *Teen Vogue* duct tape dress with flowery straps this morning and I've had over eighty hits. Not to mention tons of comments, some with questions that needed responses!

So instead of retesting my original hypothesis, I think I'll go back to step one.

THE SCIENTIFIC METHOD

Step 1: Ask a Question

Question: Will Chip and I still be together when we start eighth grade next fall?

Now *there's* a topic I can throw myself into researching!

Yours in Luck and Love,

Kara McAllister

Acknowledgments

I'd like to thank my parents for providing me with a childhood full of books, and all of the other important things in life. And thank you, too, to those who live with me now – my husband, son, and daughter – for never complaining about the crazy kind of household kept by one who uses every free minute for writing instead of vacuuming, folding clothes, or any of the other unimportant things in life. Thank you to my wonderful friend Joy Purcell, for reading the first draft when I needed it in a hurry. And thanks to the fabulous Sudipta Bardhan-Quallen, whose phone calls, advice, and laughter kept me writing through the tough times. I owe a huge thanks to my agent, Rosemary Stimola, who "saw a spark" and then waited over a year for it to flame. It takes many talented people to create a book, so I'd like to thank the entire team at Scholastic, especially Whitney Lyle, Cheryl Weisman, and Kevin Callahan. Tremendous gratitude goes to my brilliant editor, Aimee Friedman, whose keen vision for THE BOY PROJECT helped me take Kara's story from good to überfuntastic.

About the Author

Kami Kinard enjoys writing about the boyfriend quest more than she enjoyed experiencing it. She is currently a teaching artist on the South Carolina Arts Commission's Roster of Approved Artists to serve in arts education programs across the state. Kami writes from Beaufort, South Carolina, where she lives with her husband and two children. Please visit her online at www.kamikinard.com.